Adarsh Rumba

ISBN 979-8-89475-004-0

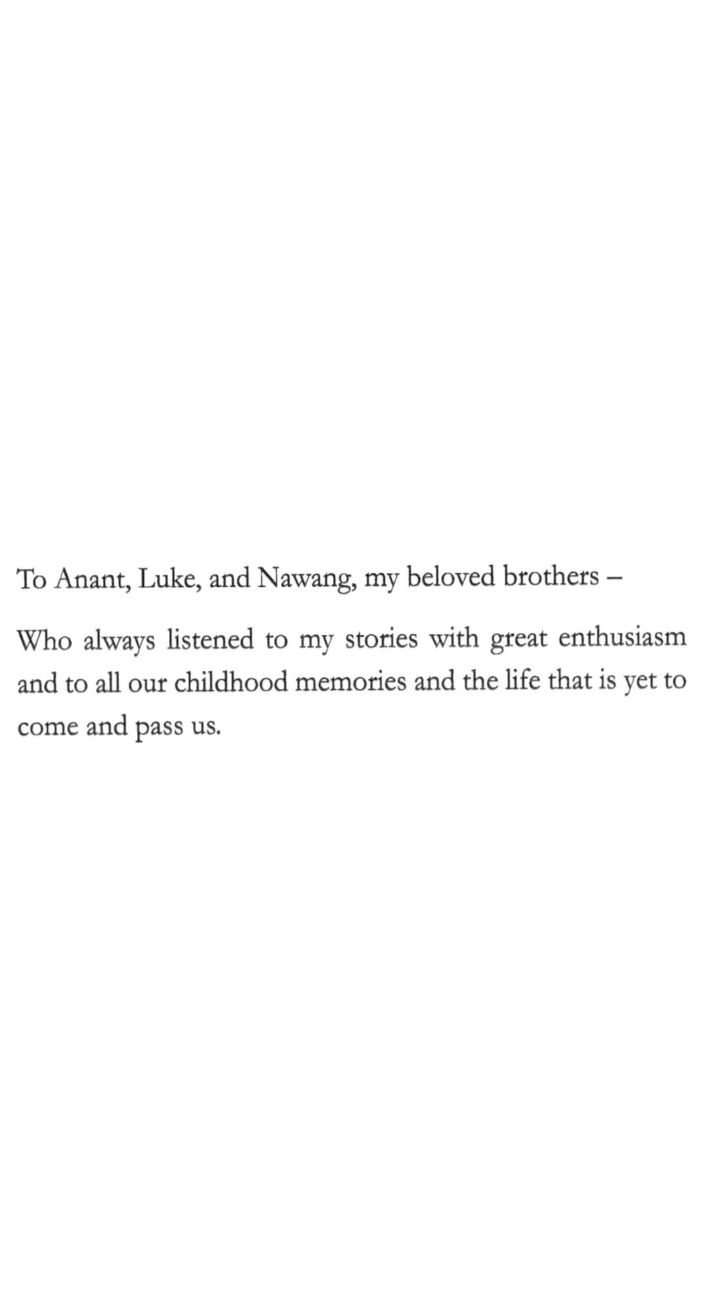

To Anant, Luke, and Nawang, my beloved brothers –

Who always listened to my stories with great enthusiasm and to all our childhood memories and the life that is yet to come and pass us.

CONTENTS

PREFACE

"We suffer more often in imagination than in reality."

— Seneca

That is a very profound thought indeed. I would humbly seek to refute the great philosopher to the best of my capacity with my humble creation.

I'm a man of belief that colourful contemplation is a byproduct of leisure, a gift to us as cognitive beings. We are gifted with the power to think, and in thought, we might paint the best of our fantasies. Therefore, we at times also, rejoice in our untimely contemplation.

With the above note, I'd like to proudly present to you a collection of my original short stories, which, at times, stirs up the distinction between fiction and reality. However, it seeks to present itself as an authentic reflection of the hill society, as the story revolves in and around the people of Darjeeling. I genuinely implore, this collection, fetches you hope in the dark, joy and laughter when you're feeling low, and ultimately strength to cry or weep when you are feeling heavy!

As humans, we must evoke and face all the shades of emotions, as stoicism might not be the only champion to save us from the turmoil of modern times!

With this, I would gladly like to invite you to my little world.

Happy reading!

P.S. - VIVAMUS, MORIENDUM EST

HARKAMAN

Aman carrying at least a tonne of grass on his back climbed down the riverfront of the Railing River. Making his way to his hut, which was the last house of the village, constructed out of red mud, hay, and bamboo, with windows slightly larger than the modern-day ventilator. He lived a fairly simple life in a small village that strategically fell between two towns, namely Kainjale and Sukhia, sharing one-third of its border with a completely different nation. A country that was believed to be ruled by the incarnation of Lord Vishnu himself, Nepal! The nation of brave and legendary warriors and the former land of Lord Buddha.

Harkaman Bahadur Gurung, a man probably in his mid-twenties who did not speak much, was renowned for his brute strength and bravery. There was a canard amongst the villagers that he was cursed. Thus, he was often boycotted from the ceremonial functions, and people mostly avoided talking to him. As the rumours had it, villagers believed he was a henchman to a powerful witch; therefore, he ate human flesh as a ritualistic practice. Furthermore, it was believed that Harkaman had once killed a bear with his bare hands. Some even suggested that he had the strength and stamina of ten horses because he never got tired, and nobody ever caught him resting.

A man surrounded by anecdotes that arose because of his abnormally greyish pupil, and he could only see the world in two shades, black and white. Other arrays of colours were unknown to him. A well-built man with an approximate height of 6'3ft, an abnormal height for his ethnic background. His voice sounded as though it had been fermented under a hundred coverings. The kids would throw stones at him, thinking that he was blind. He did not like kids or other people from his village; they would only speak to him in times of their need. He did have a soft corner for animals, but he never felt the need for a friend.

The other side of the Railing River was his favourite place for his cattle fodder, as others were too scared of the ghost sightings, while some believed the land on the other side to be sacred. A home to the forest Goddess. Those who were brave enough were too lazy to go to the other side, as it was an uphill climb of at least four kilometres, prior to just making it to the bank of the river, he would always go the extra mile.

Grasses on the other side of the river would never cease to end; rather, they would grow at double the pace of what regular grass would! Not only this, but sheep would produce better wool, and cows would produce dense milk. It seemed the grass had some kind of nutritious value to it. Beyond those enigmatic grass fields lay an immensely dense forest, undisturbed by humankind, a jungle so dense that it would make it almost impossible for the rays of the sun to penetrate the abyss, even at midday.

Harkaman had been pretty much alone after his grandmother left him in this ironically bright world! She died of a heart attack, in the modern medical understanding, as she often complained about the numbness in her left hand and pain in the right side of her torso. Although the witch-doctor's final verdict was that she was struck by the "*Hunter God's arrow*", Harkaman was just a boy when she passed away. Therefore, he was a man with no family.

Sheru, the canine, kept him company; he was a smart dog, with a white furry coat with a few patches of black. His ears would always be pointed towards the sky, especially when he saw Harkaman. Sheru never forgot to wiggle his tail every time Harkaman returned from his ventures. Sheru never seemed biased, and he always welcomed him without any expectations. This small world seemed big for both of them, and the only things that mattered to them were each other's company. But today, when Harkaman lay down his load of grass, neither did he see Sheru waiting outside his hut to wiggle his glorious tail in celebration of Harkaman's return, nor did he hear any barking from the shed below his hut.

This uncertain behaviour of his friend surprised him, but he did not pay much attention to it, thinking that Sheru would return by night. Something similar had happened a few months prior when Sheru had reached the neighbouring village, as he chased down the cat that tried to steal from them. Besides, he was way too hungry to bother about the whereabouts and other details. It was all the same for Harkaman as for all the other Gurkhas; one thing he distinctly remembered was that his grandmother used to say:

"Kam sachey afulai, khanu sache aru lai."

…meaning if you try to procrastinate on your work, you will eventually have to do it alone, but if you procrastinate eating your meal, someone else would come and have it instead! His neighbour 'Kallu' would always show up before his lunch or supper time and wouldn't leave until he was offered something to eat.

Harkaman hurriedly sneaked inside his hut and shut the door behind him. He sat down, pulling a *murda* near his *chula*, pulling the firewood from above it, and started a spark by striking two white rocks against each other. The dried hay finally caught a spark, raising smoke, and he began blowing into the smoke to kindle the fire, blowing away white smoke with *sotey*. He coughed as he blew, meanwhile placing the shapeless cooking pot filled with rice porridge, a leftover from his breakfast. He pulled the smoked beef meat that hung above the chula, as he was too tired to cook. As he placed the first handful of rice in his mouth, he heard Kallu approaching his hut, the same Kallu who wore a tatty *Parde-topi* and a shabby brownish *Dhaura sural,* which might have been grey in some distant past. He always sang in his thin, nosy, off-scale voice and would claim that he once performed for the King in Nepal. No wonder he landed in a place like that. Harkaman hogged as fast as he could, stuffing his face to the fullest capacity of his mouth. Alas, Kallu made it to his door.

"Aaaeee Ha-ur-kaie, I just saw you coming, thought I'd just say hello."

Harkaman stuffed his face with what remained on his plate and took the last shred of dried meat that remained in his hand. He stood up, quietly chewing on the meat, stuck in a dilemma, whether he should open the door or sneak out from the window.

He then pulled out his khukuri and snuck out the window to seek his loyal friend Sheru. He took a small bottle of kerosene, packed some *dhero* in a cloth and, pulling another strand of dried meat in his sling bag, he quietly sneaked out the window, shutting it behind him from outside. Kallu grew impatient and started to bang louder. As he stood there for a long time without any answer, in great disappointment, he yelled,

"Hare Hare! There is no point in being good to your neighbours these days!"

Harkaman was long gone and was now looking for Sheru. He inquired to quite a few villagers who were sceptical and scared of him, but they all denied seeing Sheru. Harkaman recalled that he had last spotted Sheru near the river, where he had to pelt at Sheru to send him back. Harkaman bought some kerosene for 5 paise per 500ml, along with matches for 1 ana. He pulled out an old cloth out of his bag and then tied it tightly around the stick, and poured the kerosene from the top of the cloth, all the while rotating the stick from left to right. The sun was already bidding farewell to the world and Harkaman. He looked towards the sky before he started his venture and thought to himself, at least we are under the same black sky.

He then struck the matchstick and lit the torch, then carefully crossed the river. Somehow, the water seemed to be deeper than the time he crossed the river earlier. He could feel the water pushing against him. He held the bag on his head and walked towards the other side. He felt something slithering between his feet. He tried to shake it away, but it stayed with him until he crossed the river as though the unknown sought to guide him across the river. He checked his feet and lit the flame torch for a closer inspection into the water, yet failed to notice anything out of the ordinary.

Harkaman strapped his bag on his left shoulder, clenched the khukuri in his right palm, and placed the torch above his head with his left hand, lighting the way, carefully inspecting the ground ahead of him with his bare feet, simultaneously keeping alert for any unfamiliar shapes, sounds, and beats that resided in the dark. He called his friend's name;

"Sheru, come, boy, the house awaits, Sheru, Sheru."

There was only pitch darkness and the momentary creaks of the branches in return, ripples of his voice dissolving into the void ahead. He had almost reached the other side, crossing the grass fields, the farthest he had ever gone.

Harkaman now stood under magnificently tall trees that engulfed the darkness and hollow of the abyss. Strange noises came from the woods, as if someone screamed, as the wind passed by the magnificently large trees. The further he went, the more peaceful it became a sense of stillness, a dead stillness that haunted him. An epiphany of the delusional concept of peace struck Harkaman.

The world around him stood still, with a constant scent of wet soil and moss. Darkness stared upon him quietly, patiently, but with great anger and envy. Although Harkaman enjoyed the quietness, a constant gaze from behind the trees concerned him. He turned towards the direction and demanded with an authoritative voice;

"Who are you? Come forth and show yourself!"

He waited in both suspicion and curiosity, only to turn back in disappointment. Not paying much attention, he continued his climb towards the direction at a snail's pace, piercing the blanket of silence with brittle vibrations that followed with each step he took on that wild mattress of twigs and small branches.

A sudden pounding of his heart felt as though it would fall out on his palms. The air just seemed thicker, consisting of that wet, unusual smell. Despite all this moist and thick atmosphere, his instincts were spiking. He held his stainless khukuri, clenching it with an iron grip. His hands were firmly locked in the striking position as he went nearer to uncloak the unknown hiding behind the dark. A distant cry pierced the ghostly stillness of the night, accompanied by a few feeble barks and a loud, painful whining. *It was Sheru, it had to be Sheru*, his loyal and only companion.

He sprung towards the direction, baffled by the absence of the unseen! He began to search for Sheru rigorously. It had to be there, the unknown presence he felt that trailed all the way here. He wondered if he was beginning to hallucinate. His inspection was yet again interrupted by an agonising scream and a pair of glittery eyes at a distance that glared at him.

Yes, he thought this was no doubt the same being that followed him throughout the forest! Those same eyes that chased Harkaman. He ran towards them; the closer he got towards them, the further they seemed. He now bled profusely from the lacerations on his feet, which sent crippling pain to his head through his spine, but he kept moving forward.

A labyrinth of tall woods and shadow, the stars that guided him a while ago were no more visible. The whole woods stood still, as though time had been frozen and the ambience instilled back to its normality, where the only sign of life seemed to be Harkaman's own heavy breathing. He took the flame torch and checked his left foot. It had been damp with blood, with multiple cuts. A particular point ached the most. As he felt it, he came to know a piece of the stick had pierced his flesh and was stuck inside.

Harkaman pinned the flame torch on the ground, keeping it upright, bit on the khukuri's handle, and took a deep breath. He then plucked it with a single pull. He squealed in agony, his blood-stained hand shaking with the crippling pain that struck his head and went in waves through his spine. The only form of first-aid that he was taught by his grandmother was to burn a cloth and place it on the wound, further securing it with another cloth. To do so, he first tore the pocket caps off his waistcoat, ripping it to shreds.

He then lit the piece of cloth and dabbed it in his palm to prevent the cloth from burning completely. He then placed the hot cloth on the wound, pressing it deeper to avoid further bleeding. He squealed in pain as he secured it with his 'patuki', falling backwards in a dramatic fashion. His body had finally given up! An unexpected hoot of an owl began at a distance with every breath he took. The world around him seemed darker, and his head began to spin. It was all but darkness at the end, the pandemonium seemed to have finally come to an end as the abyss gently embraced him. All fell silent again. Finally, he had finished bandaging himself when he was taken aback by a loud cry of a woman. Something heavy fell on his head, and he lost his consciousness.

Half-conscious with the crippling pain, he lay and felt as though he was being dragged by something huge. With immense blood loss and blurry vision, he could only make out a silhouette of a monstrous being holding his leg as he was being dragged. Harkaman did not resist and played dead. His flame torch and khukuri were nowhere to be seen. The cries got louder; at times, it even sounded like a swine. It was at this moment that he felt fear for the first time in his life. His dawra-surwal was tattered and covered in blood and dirt.

The enormous figure finally stopped at the end of a lake with a large platform-like boulder at the edge with a huge fire lit atop. He barely saw this as his eyes were still adjusting to the light. A woman, stripped bare naked, was tied to a log that was placed upright. It looked as though she had been through a lot of pain, as there were gashes all over her body. Sheru yelped helplessly as his paws were cut off. Perhaps the end was the only beginning of Harkaman's suffering. The figures moved left to right, mumbling some incantations in an enigmatic manner. Harkaman tried to lift himself up; however, his body failed to cope.

Harkaman was lifted and forced on his knees at the edge of the boulder. One of the figures, wearing a wolf coat, held Harkaman by his hair to keep his head from moving, and the other one lifted the axe. Harkaman's heart raced at the face of death. All the memories of the time he had spent with his grandmother and Sheru played in front of him, and the pain of every little animal he had savoured for food reflected in him. Moments before the heavy blade rested on his neck, the lady screamed with a gurgling voice while blood gushed out of her throat, but loud enough to echo through the forest;

"May my powers be with the one with a pure and brave-hearted soul."

The accusers were taken aback. Harkaman saw those pairs of eyes that stalked him. They glittered with rage, twinkled with a smirk, and blinked from the abyss beneath as though they invited him. Harkaman conjured the final ounce of strength and fought back, ultimately slipping and falling into the murky water of the lake.

The fall rather felt like a soft bed, made out of feathers perhaps. The slithery thing that guided him engulfed him and pulled him deeper and deeper. The warmth of the flames gradually faded and ultimately vanished. Soon, all resided in darkness. He, indeed, had been engulfed by the abyss. His pain and suffering were gone. There was silence, stillness, peace. He was suspended nowhere. The sensation of falling subsided. His mind was empty, and he lay at the centre of it all, he who had become with no form or name.

Wounds from his previous conflicts and pain had been healed. He resurfaced, hovering over the water. The two beings that sought to slaughter him a while ago now bowed down to him and were blown away by the wind as he gestured with his palm. The sun arose, gradually filling the pitch-black sky with fresh shades of orange, blue, and red. The forest seemed cleansed and fresh, greener than ever. He with no name could now witness it all. He saw it all, he felt it all. He became nature, he was the abyss, he was everything…

Opening his eyes, the same pair of red eyes, he said…

"I know it all. I'm everything and nothing."

WINTER RUSH

"**C**HEEEEER!!"

Tall, fizzy glasses filled up to the brim clashed together as the three friends yelled!

"Congratulations! I'm so happy for you, Benjamin. Such short notice, but I'm genuinely happy for you…"

"Congratulations, comrade. Enjoy your last beer with your friends. It's all going to be requests and begging once you get married!"

"Thank you, guys. I'm so glad that we could catch up today!"

"Of course, after all, tomorrow is a big day!"

"Oh! Come on, Shiwani, stop saying 'big day' as if it's something grand. Tomorrow is a sad day, for it's a 'lamb to the slaughter.'"

They all laughed heartily, for the three friends finally had a chance to meet after almost half a decade. It's strange that we chase our dreams so vigorously that we forget to keep track of who's left behind in this everlasting chase. The group of five had, strangely enough, cut down to a mere group of triplets. Vasudha was married and settled elsewhere, and Dilip had joined the army and couldn't make it as he was posted in Jammu, getting leaves was close to impossible. Shiwani had become a teacher at the very school where they all had once studied and shared their bittersweet memories, West Point School, Dali. Benjamin was now a manager at the State Bank of India (S.B.I.), and lastly, Tenzi had a travel business of his own.

The uncertainty of life took all the friends away from their desired destinations, eventually forcing them to part ways. Life and nuances are comic. Similar to Sir Indra Bahadur Rai's short story *'KHEER.'* The story follows a group of people trying to create an Indo-Nepal dessert. The entire conversation is built around the making, texture, and taste of an ideal kheer. However, an ironic note is heard when the dessert is completed. *"Hait, yo tha doodh bhat ani chini jasto vayesa!" (this tastes like milk and rice with sugar)*. In the end note, Sir Rai hilariously delivers the metaphor by correlating it to life, with a recipe for kheer and the actual struggle to create an ideal life.

In a mere five years, the inseparable friends dispersed in the stream of time. When the opportunity struck, only three of them could make it to Joey's Pub with full glasses and half-hearted smiles.

It seemed as if life had a speeding effect on them. They spoke of their school and college days, how they used to bunk classes to go for movies and dates. With Benjamin on the lookout, as he had been single ever since they met him. "As the alcohol goes in, the truth comes out," rightfully said.

Benjamin began to laugh out loud. He never indulged in drinking during his college days. Hence, it got to him first. Shiwani and Tenzi, both caught by surprise, looked at their friend with astonishment. Benjamin was so loud that the staff had to ask him to keep it low since the other guests were getting disturbed.

Shiwani: *"Is everything okay? What's so funny? Tell us as well."*

Benjamin, unable to answer, shook his head from right to left, blotting red like a happy pufferfish.

Tenzi: *"Let him enjoy being a poor fellow, after all…"*

Shiwani: *"What is wrong with you? Weren't you the one who used to preach love in school days, although you had become a sadistic pain in the ass by the time you reached college?"*

"Exactly!" said Benjamin, still gasping for air as he choked with his giggles.

Shiwani: *"We know you have gone through a bad breakup lately. That doesn't give you a licence to be mean and rude to others!"*

Tenzi, not paying much attention, took the last sip of his beer and called for another one, gesturing with a raised finger:

Tenzi: *"A Scotch, please! Hey guys, guys, guys! Come on now, stop it. It's me just trying to induce some humour in our mundane lives. Mundane lives… Cheers to it!"*

Benjamin lifted his glass, *"I believe that is what we have made out of our lives!"*

His cheeks had started picking up the heat from the alcohol, his drowsy eyes and his neatly ironed formals slowly crumbling to shreds along with loosened ties. Shiwani just observed the two men. One could make out her sparkling, judgemental looks, specifically a disgusted one, filled with sarcasm and hurtful words if bestowed upon. She held those words, but her wide hazel eyes spoke them out loud.

Although she kept a perfect posture and tried her best to conceal with her calm smile, she would have definitely blasted those two men if they were still in college, even worse if they were in school. Tenzi did notice and thought to himself, 'She has mellowed down a lot, maybe because she is a teacher now.' He tried to keep this thought to himself. He also discovered she had a mole above the upper right side of her lips, and her hair was now straight; they used to be wavy. However, the alcohol didn't let him. He stared at her for two straight minutes or so and only realised when he was poked by Shiwani's question.

Shiwani: *"Hello! Mr. Bhutiya! What are you staring at?"*

Benjamin: *"I think he is charmed by you like he used to be back at school…"*

Barely lifting his head, Benjamin added, then he went back to his heads-down position, giggling, just like in their school days.

Tenzi: *"Don't mind him. He is a bit drunk."*

Shiwani: *"I asked you a question. Don't get ideas; it's not going to happen!"*

Tenzi: *"Where did that come from now?"*

Shiwani: "*I know you men are all the same! If a girl smiles at you and talks to you nicely, you all take it as a green signal to get laid with her, isn't it?*"

Tenzi: "*It's nothing like that. Come on now, don't escalate the mere subject. Are you even in your senses? I believe it's a bit too much, so let's call it a night! Let me drop you both home, okay? Excuse me, sir, could you get us our bill, please?*"

Tenzi reached out for his wallet…

Shiwani: "*It's okay to keep your money to yourself. I don't need your sympathy, nor do I need your help. I can manage on my own.*"

Tenzi just smiled and replied, "*In that case, please be my guest!*"

Shiwani: "*Don't act so cool. How shameful of you to make a lady pay alone?*"

Tenzi: "*I said you are welcome to pay your bill. I never determined who. I do not understand what has been bothering you, but see it's not very right on your part to generalise men.*"

Shiwani: "*Generalise? Don't you all beg and chase women like dogs? Once she gives her body and soul to you, all you do is despise her and disrespect her.*"

Breaking into tears, she screamed at the top of her voice, only to realise the whole pub was staring at their table. She felt embarrassed and ran out, grabbing her mint green tote bag that perfectly matched her pearl blue overcoat. Tenzi woke Benjamin, cleared their bill, and left calmly. He politely apologised to the staff for causing them trouble.

Although he felt the urgency to run after Shiwani, he took his time gathering himself and his drunk friend. Darjeeling can be pretty cold, even in February. Although the summer (disguised monsoon) was right around the corner, Tenzi felt the cold winds biting him down his spine the moment they stepped outside Joey's Pub.

He then ran up to the Gymkhana Club stand to get his green Bolero and picked up Benjamin, who lay like a sack of potatoes on the staircase of Dragon Market, a miniature mall with two pillars at its entry gate, red dragons carved on each of them, decorated with green scales on their back swirling up towards the sky. A place where you can buy all the fancy clothes and gadgets, a place where the rich ones go to shop.

If you are lucky enough, you will probably spot a kid named Aieté. He stares inside through the huge glass pane of the *Arsenal store*, looking at all the fancy action figures, clothes, and shoes with his bright and beautiful eyes. He himself burdened with responsibilities and the luggage of visitors from around the world who came to witness the beauty of the 'Queen of Hills.' It's a miracle how one could bear so much weight on their young shoulders. He stands there every now and then, sometimes barefoot, sometimes with a pair of old, oversized flip-flops, patched multiple times, mostly invisible to the people of this beautiful town.

Tenzi purposely took the longer route, by detouring Goinka petrol pump and stopping near the Gum stand. Packed with people throughout, it's almost impossible to get into a cab during tourist season because even if you manage to get one, local aunties wouldn't let you get in. They would probably push you off with their shopping bags. Looking for Shiwani, meanwhile many people came to his vehicle's window, some even tried getting in.

"Ghum?"

"Does this vehicle go to Ghum?"

He denied it with a forced smile and a left-to-right head gesture until he saw her. He moved his car near her, lowering the window pane:

Tenzi: *"Please get in, this vehicle goes to 'Batasia.' It's a special service, just for the day!"*

Shiwani, who still shivered with cold or maybe anger, avoided looking in the direction. It had started drizzling gently, and the taxi driver behind Tenzi's car kept honking. She, too, knew she had a slim chance of getting a cab anytime soon. She got into the vehicle and slammed the second seat door angrily behind her.

Tenzi just smiled and twisted the key. Hardly had they moved and reached 'the Darjeeling Railway station' when they were stuck in a traffic jam. A huge army truck, referred to as a *"Shaktiman"* by the locals, refused to back down, and a Mazda had nowhere else to go. An uneasy silence engulfed them, with occasional honks in between. Benjamin had far gone to his sweet dreams, smiling even in his sleep. Maybe he dreamt of himself preparing for marriage, as it was a big day for him tomorrow.

It began to shower outside, and the frozen droplets broke on the roof of the vehicle, the ones that probably came before it snows, smaller in size but greater in number. Now the drivers began to honk even more in fear of getting stuck all night inside their vehicles.

Shiwani: "*Great, now I'm stuck inside this box with two men!*"

Tenzi: "*I'm stuck inside with this hothead! We are your friends, by the way. Don't be so distant, will you?*" Looking at the reflection in the rearview mirror, he reciprocated.

Shiwani: "*You men think it's very easy to get inside a woman's pants, don't you? Especially you, stop your nonsensical blabbering.*"

Tenzi felt outraged and took a deep breath. He calmed himself down and said:

"*Will you please tell me what happened? I know you are generally a hothead and like bullying me, but I feel you are not yourself today. If you think I'm forcing you to come along, then I'll probably help you transition to another cab, but please stop treating me like a punching bag. I'm still your friend, who is just trying to make conversation for old times' sake!*"

Shiwani: "*You mean the time you said you liked me? Is that the old time you were talking about?*"

Tenzi: "*For GOD'S SAKE, SHIWANI, what is wrong with you? Don't tell me you are still mad at me regarding that!*"

Shiwani: "*That's not it, but it's funny how you men think it's easy to walk in and out of anyone's life. You all talk about feelings, 'fake feelings.' The only real deal about you is that lust you carry around. That is who you all are!*"

Tenzi: "*Firstly, please stop generalising! What would you know about what men go through? We live in a society that has been structured in such a manner that if a man expresses his feelings, he is either being weak or a fake!*"

Shiwani: "*You don't even start with problems, Mr. Tenz-ee Bhutia! Do you go around bleeding from between your legs, still having to go to work like nothing happened? For your information, we live in the same society that thinks women should not roam around late at night, that is, post 6:00 p.m.!*"

Tenzi: "*Well, the 'period.'*

Yes, you are pretty right; I wouldn't want to go around all the while bleeding from my genitals and, on top of having all those hormonal imbalances. Shiwani, I might not exactly know what it feels like, but I'm really sorry. Look, I'm not advocating that all men are good, and neither am I saying I'm the holiest! Men, too, have problems and might not be as physically or mentally punishing as women go through. But we, too, suffer from depression, anxiety, and trauma. Boys are crushed in this society and restructured to be men. It's neither of our faults; it's the type of place in which we are brought up. Boys are told that only girls and women cry; therefore, in the mask of masculinity, we lose our right towards our emotions. We are brainwashed to believe that only women cry, and crying is bad and a sign of weakness! Not only this, we are told from a very young age that someday we will have to marry a "*good woman*", one who is soft-spoken, doesn't answer back, knows how to cook, and will be easily tamed. In short, a puppet! We lose our freedom to choose.

Let's come to responsibility. Ideal men must be responsible for their actions. Sometimes, it feels like if you are born a boy, your only purpose in life is to be a crutch to your family when they need you. One loses his freedom itself. Did you know men, too, are raped? No! How would you know? It's not the hot news; it won't sell. Moreover, what would society think of you?

"You were so weak that you couldn't defend yourself, or else, it must have been fun for you…" These are the words of sympathy a male rape victim receives. If you still think we all are the same, I cannot do much, Miss Pradhan."

Pulling out a cigarette from his coat pocket. Shiwani felt a sense of calm. For the first time, someone had not given her a cold shoulder regarding periods. Besides, no one had ever spoken to her in such a manner because of her short temper. She always felt a bit distant from everyone. Vehicles started moving as the congestion in the traffic was cleared. The army man had finally agreed to step down for the greater good. The sky still looked outraged; it kept on showering hails. Tenzi broke the uneasy air inside the vehicle.

Tenzi: *"You know, I did really like you back in school, but those feelings seem to have disappeared over the years. It's just unbiased friendship that I have to offer, nothing else, and neither do I have any intent to slip my hands inside your pants. Now that I think of it, we didn't have any closure. I don't have any grudge against you, although I felt a little bad."*

Silence filled itself again and took the shape of the vehicle itself. Shiwani was thinking something. She kept quiet and was fixated on the mist outside, entangled in her unclear thoughts. It felt as though she had drawn up a wall against the whole wide world once again, the cold world that wanted a piece of her the moment she stepped out! They were stopped by the traffic police near Marry Resort. Random checks often took place. Good thing the police was an old friend. Shiwani waited inside the car as she carefully drew something on the glass with her spongy, squishy hands and those perfectly self-manicured fingernails. Tenzi somehow felt that it would be warm inside that bubble, but he dared not step in after what had happened. He got in the car and started the engine. Shiwani stared at him, snapping out of her reverie.

"Done already?" She seemed to be a different person this time, a sense of calm and kindness entwined in her tone.

Tenzi: *"Yes, ma'am!"*

Shiwani: *"Tenz-ee…"*

Tenzi: *"Hhmm…"*

Shiwani: *"Can I sit in the front seat? The second seat feels a bit lonely and dark."*

Tenzi: *"Haha, but Benjamin is strapped right beside you!"*

Shiwani: *"Yes, but he is asleep. It's okay if you are mad at me. I'll sit here."*

Tenzi: *"No, no, not at all. Please hop in."*

Shiwani: *"Tenz-ee…"* Breaking the silence, for the first time in the entire evening, she genuinely smiled, just like in their school days.

"Yes…" still focused on his driving, all this while pulling out another cigarette and placing it on his lips.

Shiwani: "May I ask you a question?"

Tenzi: "Shoot…"

Shiwani: "Why did you propose to me in the first place?"

The vehicle stopped with a screech as Tenzi stepped on the brake, and slipping on the wet roads, his vehicle stopped a few metres ahead of 'Tara Devi' temple. He turned his head slowly towards her. His heart knocked loudly against his rib cage, almost begging him to come out, and it was as if he was taken back in time, a rush of adrenaline. Pupils dilated, he broke a sweat although his vehicle's digital thermometer reflected -1°C outside.

He awkwardly tried to force a smile, just like that day, and he brought both his hands up, covering his cheeks. *"You won't slap me again, will you?"*

Shiwani burst into laughter. While still confused, Tenzi tried laughing with her, with his guard held high, tried coping with the joke and the pace of time that had gone by. Although it was warm inside, it began to snow. The clouds let go of all the weight they carried, and people began to come out and scream with joy. Thus, this invisible bubble did feel warm to Tenzi as his high school sweetheart hugged him. All this while, Benjamin had his lights out. Breathing in his ears, Shiwani asked:

"Was it because you thought we both were different, in the same way?"

Meanwhile, somewhere in "*Shiva gram,*" next to the polluted stream, Aieté looked for a wooden plank to fix the broken roof of his ten by fifteen excuse of a cold room made of tin and wood, where he would sleep on the floor as his sick mother lay on the bed.

NAME?

Murmuring in his subdued and half-conscious voice, he rubbed his eyes and sluggishly tilted towards the edge of his bed. Vaguely recalling his misty dream and wondering to himself,

'That was a weird dream...'

In fact, his preposterous words barely made sense to himself. In an effort to make literal sense or at least try not to forget the phrase, he repeated under his breath:

"PINK SKY, WHISKEY-RED LIPS, HEAVENLY EYES, COULD SHE BE AN ANGEL IN DISGUISE?"

Meanwhile, pandiculating, he peered at the table clock. 08:07 am, now flickered to 08:08 am; Prabin hurled his blanket and sprung off, grabbed his towel, and stormed towards the bathroom. Letting out a yawp, he quivered. The water felt fine after some time, not as cold as before. In no time, he walked out of the bathroom rubbing his wet hair and picked his phone.

3 missed calls and two messages!

The screen lit up along with these notifications as soon as the device recognised his fingers. He tossed his phone and ran towards his wardrobe to change. At the corner of his bed at an asymmetrical angle stood a tall old wooden wardrobe that directly faced the entrance to his room. Prabin, while still deciding what to wear, heard his phone ring for the fourth time; *Ping!*'

Dhiren: "*Dude, I hope you are ready. I'll come pick you up in five minutes, just leaving my house.*"

"*Give me a breather for God's sake, bub!*"

Talking to himself, he then ran his hands all over his body, as well as activating all his senses…

"*Keys check! Wallet check! (A quick sniff) Perfume check!*"

Scanning the whole room that looked more like a dump yard than an actual room, with packets of chips littered and tossed clothes, which were probably a result of hasty decision-making, surprisingly clean white walls with a poster of him and a fairly middle-aged pretty lady with her arms around him from a time long forgotten. Now, he hardly had any time, and the restaurant kept his mother busy.

Crystal clean windows. From those clean windows, a view of majestic Kangchenjunga, *Five Treasures of the Great Snow*' in its literal Tibetan tongue, sitting atop like a crown. It felt as though the windows were thoroughly cleaned only for this particular purpose. Every time Prabin looked out from his window, it would transfix him, and as he entered a state of utmost euphoria, an onset to his unorthodox rumination would sway Prabin. He would imagine himself flying, enduring cold breezes on his temple and his soft, neatly shaved cheeks, and wished that he could even teleport himself to those white, soft, snow-covered mountains. Who knows, he might even encounter a Yeti to his fat luck.

Too imaginative and ambitious for a twenty-five-year-old man indeed, 'but those were his thoughts and his alone, and no one could possibly mould them', for Prabin believed *'it was very important to be practical, but one must keep that inner child entertained.'* He snapped out of his reverie as he received another text from Dhiren.

Alas, there lay the toughest of tasks at hand, to sneak out for the day by crossing the dining hall under his mother's nose. He slowly unplugged his charging phone from the socket and quietly leapt towards the door!

Mother: *Prabin…*

Prabin: *Bye, Ama, I'm leaving!*

As he rushed towards the main door, he was caught off guard, and he felt a sudden pull from behind. He carefully tilted his head towards the rear of his shoulder as slowly as he could, recalling his childhood memories. The narrative remained unchanged even after all those years. Behind him stood his mother, nurturing and paramount. Holding him by the bag, almost strangling him with one hand and a rolling pin in the other.

Mother: *You will not leave the house without having your breakfast!*

Prabin: *...But, Ama, I'm already late!* (helplessly)

Her classic mother's glare supplemented in acquiring his approval.

"*Yes, Ama...*" Prabin with a grumpy face.

Dhiren: *Prabin, did you die while applying your makeup, or did you just wake up late, you lazy bum?*

Dhiren came in, roaring in his swagger through the main gate, and made his way to the hallway's door. As he entered the hall and turned at the sight of Prabin's mother, his voice metamorphosed to a mere squeak of a rat. Dhiren had lost his parents at a young age and was brought up by his uncle. Therefore, he always regarded Prabin's mother with respect.

Dhiren: Namaste, Auntie. How have you been?

Shifting his glances towards Prabin...

Dhiren: *Prabin, why do you have to wake up so late? It's okay, finish your breakfast. I'll be waiting here.*

While passing a quick gesture towards the door and innocently smiling back at Prabin's mother, all this while, none of this had gone unnoticed.

"*Namaste, come and join him, Dhiren.*"

"*Actually, Auntie...*"

"*Are you sure?*"

"*There is always space for one or two parathas, haha...*"

The breakfast passed pretty much in silence, only with quite a few exchanges in between. A typical army man's house, where you don't get to talk unless you have been asked to.

"Here is the list of things from the market I want you to get, and here's the money for the groceries. Try and come early today as you will be going back tomorrow. I'll cook something special."

Kissing his ama on her cheek, Prabin picked up his bag. Dhiren kicked Prabin as they left the house. Prabin turned, grabbed his friend in a wrestler's grip, and kicked him as well. The two men laughed their hearts out on the way, taking a trip down memory lane, refreshing their memory from school days. Kanchenjunga smiled back at them, just the way it used to, but now from the nook and corner of the unplanned tall buildings…

In no time, they reached the main town. Prabin parked his bike in front of the Rink mall, now better referred to as 'THE BIG BAZAAR'. People of Darjeeling mostly visit more to benefit from the clean and 'free' washrooms that the mall provides rather than anything else. A taxi stopped at a frog hair's breadth to Prabin. He turned and was about to yell at the driver, but the second seat window started to roll down gracefully.

Bringing into view a lady with a palely tan complexion, aviators resting atop a tall nose, pierced on the right side with a fairly thin silver ring, a carmine-shaded pair of lips that looked as if they would melt if one were to touch them gently, and straight dense locks of hair, to over-dramatise, as dark as the night sky. A subtle smile on her face, such an enigmatic gaze, *"Excuse me?"* A raspy voice that would probably tickle one's soul.

"*Yes?!*" In an in-sync fashion, the boys responded!

Lady: (Chuckles) "*Could you tell us where Ladenla Road is?*"

Prabin took a deep sigh and replied, "*You are on 'the' Ladenla Road.*" Dhiren stood quiet and transfixed.

Lady: "*Oh, did not realise, thank you, and nice ride.*"

Almost as if making it up for almost running the taxi over them, Prabin almost jumped with excitement and spontaneity. Men might like women, but they love women who align with their interests a little more.

Prabin: "*Thank you. It's a Harley Davidson Street 750. We could go for a ride someday, I mean, if you want?*"

The traffic cleared before they could talk anymore, and the vehicle swiftly moved through the road. Like a dream, she just went by, she looked behind and waved at them.

Dhiren: "*You are an idiot. You should have at least taken her number.*"

Prabin: "*It's okay. She just seemed genuinely nice.*"

Dhiren: "*That's why she was checking you out and hitting on you, fool. Let's make a run for it. We can still catch up.*"

Prabin: "*Chuck it. Besides, Ama has sent a long list. For your information, it is called genuinely complimenting, not checking out! It is a small town, after all. We might bump into each other later.*"

Dhiren: "*You don't seem too interested though, all good? I know you like men, but come on, she was worth a try!*" (jokingly)

Prabin: "*Stop fooling around, you fool! She was probably just asking for directions and having some fun with you. Besides, women are a lot more than just pretty faces, probably ten times wiser than you, and she's definitely too wise for your sorry brain. In short, way out of your league!"*

"Here we go! Prince of comebacks! Okay, I give up."

As the day passed by, Dhiren gradually forgot about the lady. Blessed are those who fall easily in and out of love. However, Prabin felt as though he was struck by lightning on a bright summer day.

Prabin was certainly more than an average-looking hill person himself, tall, with a dusky complexion, neatly done hair, and a street photographer. Prabin was more of a stoic. He liked keeping to himself, did not care what others thought of him, was shy at times, quiet yet confident and calm as a lake, and often lost in himself. But he could not

shake off the peculiarity of the recent encounter. To him, the nameless lady seemed beyond ordinary. She wasn't just a pretty face but an undying and unforgettable aura, one that would emancipate one's soul.

He could not comprehend his emotions that overwhelmed him at the moment. It had been years since he had felt this way and had met such an individual of riveting disposition. Just a thought of her was enough to make him smile throughout the day.

Oh! And she was way beyond an average woman, one of a kind that Maya Angelou mentioned in her poem 'Phenomenal Woman.' It would patently take more than a few cheesy pickup lines and those stupid jokes to impress her. She was far more than quotidian, he thought to himself. A woman who would have men dropping at her feet like flies, and if attraction was a war and one was to wage it against her, they would rather surrender before they suffered any losses. For she was a personification of that poem, "*she was a woman phenomenally phenomenal!*"

The rest of the day for these two young men was spent shopping out of the list, with minor tea breaks in between. An uncanny guilt of not getting a chance to know the lady haunted Prabin all day long. It's strange how humans can contradict their own conscience, rather, cheat on it. This feeling to know her was too overwhelming for someone as sceptical as Prabin. His scepticism knew no bounds. So much so that he had the habit of smelling his newly bought socks twice before he wore them. Hence, Geoffrey Chaucer's "love at first sight" was definitely not Prabin's cup of tea. What would someone like him name this feeling, or could they deem it to be nameless?

The entire encounter came nowhere close to Rick & Ilsa's love depicted in Casablanca, a kind of love that is so intense and inseparable yet sacrifices at the end. Prabin did not have the courage to give off this 'Phenomenal Woman.' As a matter of fact, he was furtively praying to see her. Life is strange how it has a way of realigning deviances that it caused to occur in the first place.

What was this feeling? A feeling that summoned an unsettling hurricane of emotions. This feeling was neither too shallow to be referred to as an infatuation nor deep enough to be called love. Just an uneasy somewhere in between, a dilemma of thoughts and a storm of emotions. He drifted away into an unmanned train with just the two of them in it. No matter how hard he tried to keep a grip on his rumination, it would gradually drift away from him onto her. Prabin spent his day hopelessly bewitched by that nameless enchantress. He thought to himself, "Could she be thinking of me too?" Contradicting himself in his next thought, "She's possibly a busy woman," for that, he replied to himself; he was virtually exhausted by mere overthinking.

By this time, Dhiren had to shake him off his seat. "We are done with the shopping! Let's get going!"

Prabin: "*I think I'll stay back in town for a while, maybe take a saunter at Chowrasta. Can you do me a favour and take this for Ama? I'll make it back on time for dinner.*"

Dhiren: "*I'm coming with you. Besides, Ama had asked you to come early today. Now stop trying to get both of us killed, and let's rush home.*"

Prabin: "*Stop being a kid and go home. I'll take a stroll and come back in a while. I want to feel Darjeeling for one last time before I leave for work again.*"

Dhiren knew that Prabin was seeking solitude. He often did this. Dhiren shook his head in agreement, lit a cigarette, and marched towards the Dali syndicate. Prabin climbed towards Chowrasta. A place where two roads diverged, the two friends went separate ways, and who knows where and what fate awaits.

Prabin walked uphill and smiled to himself and said, "Ladenla Road, huh." He usually walked fast, but today, he seemed to have slithered all the way up to Chowrasta. He then entered Oxford and looked for a few books on the history of Darjeeling and photography. Time moved fast, yet he wanted it to slow down, almost wishing it to stop.

Next, he tried to spend some more time by sipping tea at 'Subash Da' tea stall! *Subash Da, an infamous tea maker, renowned for his bluffs more than his tea-making skills.* It was just like they used to do during college days, passing the time by throwing ridiculous questions at Subhash Da and laughing at his replies. But none of Subash Da's questions nor his witty replies went into Prabin's head. He just sat there and scanned for those tall noses and dark, ocean-like luscious hair, which was covered by a yellow floral scarf. He checked his watch a little too frequently than usual today. The time read 17:05. He paid Subash Da, wrapped up his hopes, and walked downhill. Since he had put a closure to Pandora's box, nothing held him. His feet moved faster than ever now. It was as if he snapped out of some kind of enchantment. He dashed forward with only one goal, to reach his house.

He crossed the 'Unique Sweets and Snacks' and took a 'U-turn' as if commanded by the push of a button. He went inside and demanded, "*Sir, half a kg of kaju barfi, please.*" His ama's favourite. Putting his card forward, "*How much would that be?*" "*Sir, we are really sorry, the card machine is out of service. If you could kindly pay in cash.*" Prabin checked his wallet and only had a 50 rupee bill to spare.

"Could you kindly pack that for me, please? I'll be right back." He left the shop and ran to the closest ICICI Bank ATM, where he had to wait for his turn as he checked his watch, and it read 17:17. Without paying much attention to his surroundings, he awed at the old clock tower. Two women came out, and one of them made a query to the security guard:

Lady 1: *"Sir, could you tell me where I could get some good tea and food around here?"*

"I wouldn't know, madam. We rarely go to those expensive cafés," the guard vaguely replied.

Lady 2: *"I see. I really wanted to try something different and local."*

Although the voice sounded pretty familiar, Prabin did not bother looking behind and carelessly answered, *"You should try Machhan,"* and entered the ATM. He rushed towards Unique, and the two women were still standing right there but facing the Capital Hall this time. He passed them without bothering much, but he was yet again stopped…

Lady 1: *"Excuse me? Could you kindly tell us the location of Machhan?"*

A much more familiar voice this time… It clicked! Prabin suddenly knew this voice. He had heard this voice, that raspy, crisp voice, before. It gave him goosebumps. It was just this morning that the owner of this voice had generated a whirlwind of emotions and turned his world upside down! It was that lady, the lady with a tall pierced nose, palely tan complexion, soft carmine lips, which looked even softer and ever so delicate.

He couldn't possibly stop smiling and turned slowly. To his surprise!

Lady 1: "*Hey! It's the guy with the cool bike! Small world, isn't it?*"

Prabin's jaw dropped... She seemed even prettier this time, with the streetlight from atop directly illuminating her face, making it look even more distinct and symmetrical! The slanting rays of the setting sun kissed her spotless skin. Now, the aviators were replaced by her bare hazel brown eyes, hypnotising the onlookers! Those eyes! Most beautiful of them all, no wonder she hid them with those big aviators, keeping the world safe from her petrifying gaze. Eyes ever so deep that they could even drown Kangchenjunga itself. He was caught completely off-guard and was forever lost in them!

Prabin's heart raced, almost rhythmically. He involuntarily chanted under his breath. It all made sense as he whispered, "*Pink sky, whiskey red lips, heavenly eyes, could she be an angel in disguise?*"

Lady 1: "*Sorry? I did not get you?*"

Prabin: "*My apologies. What I meant was, yes! Yes! Sure... Small world indeed.*"

Lady 1: "*So, could you guide us with the directions?*"

Prabin: "*How about I take you there?*"

Lady 2: "*You guys should go ahead. I just remembered I have a few pending chores to take care of.*"

Lady 1: "*Come on, don't be a spoilsport. They can wait, right?*" (*looking at Prabin's direction*)

Prabin: "*Yes! You should come…*" (*reluctantly*)

Lady 2: "*I suppose not. Sorry, you guys carry on for today.*"

Prabin: "*Sure! Thank you…*"

Those words spilt out of his mouth without his permission, one of those moments where you have no control over yourself and a totally cringeworthy moment. A bit surprised, both women burst out in laughter, and Prabin, blushing but mostly happy, just smiled.

Lady 2: "*You are welcome. Just make sure she reaches her home safe?*"

Prabin and the lady began to walk towards the direction of the café as her friend playfully nudged her before parting ways, as though assigning an approval and smiling at Prabin.

Lady 1: "*I hope you are free, though.*"

Prabin: "*Yes, very much, but there's one small problem!*"

Lady 1: "*What?*"

Shocked and curious, less verbally and mostly with those big, beautiful eyes, she expressed her concern.

Prabin: "*I… never got your name?*"

Lady 1: "*Uff, silly you…*"

She looked at him for a while, making Prabin nervous, gently stretched towards Prabin's ear and whispered in her breath, making him laugh. As their joyful silhouette faded with the sinking sun, making the onlookers believe not all ends are sad.

THREE DRUNK MEN

Bikash is cold as he climbs the steep road of Darjeeling, with nothing to protect his head against the cold winter wind of 2-5 degrees Celsius. A flimsy scarf and a long dark trench coat fail to guard him against the gust of wind, and cold chills run down his spine. After a long, senseless day of being polite, he went downhill to the motor stand to board the cab for Ghum. However, he received a last-minute request from his mother over the call. Thinking to himself, there seems to be no cover for one's feelings. Although on a tight budget, he grabbed a bottle of Syrah on the way back.

When he finally reached Ghum after the obscure task given to him, he looked at his wristwatch, 18:30, and yet it had already gotten dark. Winter in the hills is unforgiving. The visibility was only about half a metre, and the path ahead of him would only be visible with every step, pretty much how life goes. He lethargically walked towards his room, where one could hardly fit a single bed and a side table. Lonely, quiet, and cold, with dim yellow light emitting from a 100W bulb, his room would get darker and colder due to power outages every now and then.

Upon reaching his room, he recalled how, when younger, he would be spooked. However, now the same darkness set him into a state of calm. As if an infuriated beast fell into a state of peace when their eyes were covered, a sinister form of peace in not being able to see. A sensation that was much more familiar; guess getting old does take a toll on us after all.

Living becomes nothing but a constant pang of agony over joy, but choosing to die would be the end of a story's potential plot twist. As a result, you are neither happy nor completely sad. You are just there like a badly done egg. Suffering, trying to exist, awaiting "the plot twist" and the final answer to the question of life and death!

Growing up gets into our heads. We become saltier as the years pass. Humans have a tendency to retain more and give less. We expect so much. We suffer because we are not selfless, even though we claim to be. Thus, the toil and agony follow. We rather enclose ourselves to protect ourselves from the world. Our personality, staunch towards proving oneself right, begins to go duller, and we believe we do not matter and we become lesser. All this because we choose to believe.

Yet even in those uncanny odds, we must strive for love. Bikash had been invited for dinner at his grandmother's place and listened to her fixated descriptions about how the village used to look and anecdotes of people he did not know. He climbed down to his cold spiral metal steps and sat upright in his man-cave. He then opened the Syrah and took a sip from the bottle. How ungentlemanly of me, he thought, but he did not have the luxury of a glass. He let the wine sit on his palate and gulped it down slowly, as always.

His phone rang. It was a call from his best friend Ronit:

Ronit: "*HELLO! OE, HAPPY NEW YEAR!*" (He sounds only optimistic for a regular night)

Bikash: "*Wish you the same, boy…*"

Ronit: "*Are you awake?*"

Bikash: "*Yep…*"

Ronit: "*COOL! COME DOWN IN A WHILE. I WANT TO WISH YOU A HAPPY NEW YEAR, I'M ON MY WAY!*"

He was a bit annoyed for an instant, as he wanted to spend the night alone, indulged in a bottle of wine and scepticism, criticising objective reality, writing an article, and feeling sorry for his state. He then hurriedly put on his jacket and trousers, inserted the bottle of wine in the inner pocket of the jacket. Just with the help of streetlight, no matter how dark, the ting of light manages to enter.

He then waited by the main gate. The landlady locked it at night. After waiting for a significant amount of time, he began stargazing. The fog from earlier was blown away by the cold winds, and he wished he could fly or teleport to a habitable planet and start anew or perhaps be united with the universe and cease to exist. The human mind and its thoughts are indeed marvellous.

His reverence was disrupted with giggles and whispers, distant echoes in the darkness of the night, marking the arrival of his friends. James had tagged along. It was already 01:20 am, and they were at the gate, fools that he loved and respected. They wished him a new year again and hugged with the gate still in between. Bikash passed them the bottle, taking sips, and one of them came up with the scintillating idea of going for a walk, tipsy and loud. It must have been fatigue, mused with a few sips of the intoxicating liquid. James was the only one not drunk, but he is always high on life, or so they said.

Being drunk drastically changes your mood. Bikash asked his friends to hold the gate, and he jumped over to embark on their night walk. They spoke about their school days, how they used to drop each other until one of their mothers would get furious about it, and one had to return home alone. That story never got old. They laughed over the incident when James got into a fight, and that was the last fight he ever got into because he was so brutal that no one dared to challenge him after that. People might have assumed them to be a sadistic, jobless bunch. After all, they are just humans at the end of the day.

They walked directionless past the railway station and then the circuit house, towards Ghum Boys High School. This place was supposedly infested with drug addicts, ghosts, and wild animals—leopards to be precise. On the contrary, this was one of the best places for a lonely dark night filled with stars, sheltered by the tall pine trees on one side. Ronit had never encountered three of the above; what he did encounter were countless sunsets and sunrises, never the same yet equally beautiful.

Today was different. It was 2 am, and he was with his two best friends, sipping and sharing wine from the same bottle, discussing trauma and laughing about it.

James: *"You know you're turning into a manga villain when you start laughing at each other's trauma."*

Ronit: *"Everyone in the group needs therapy, and the best part of it is that we all are aware, but we are too cool, so we laugh about it."*

Wine got over, so did the talk, for a moment, and then the three men walked under the stars with a temperature of three degrees Celsius. One of them farted, and to make it worse, James added, *"Cold and potatoes don't go well, do they?"* All of them burst out laughing. The three men decided to head back, and they seemed significantly drunk. Before they knew it, they were at Ronit's doorstep, dropping him off first, followed by James, and Bikash headed towards his solitude.

On the way back, he got ambushed by the street dogs. His first thought upon the sight of a pack of dogs was, *'Shit! I need to go back to work in less than three days.'* He almost got bitten by one, but as he shouted at them and pretended to pick up a rock, the dogs went docile.

He gazed at his step and moved back slowly in a very subtle manner, and walked away in the other direction, an over-thinker with impulsive behaviour at times. A part of him wanted to sprint, but past experience compelled him to remain calm. Humans often suffer more in thought, even when they don't have to in material existence. Moving forth, he picked up two large rocks, just in case, and continued his walk. The dogs did not follow, and the night felt lonely and silent again.

Past the streetlights, upon arrival at the gate, it seemed to Bikash as though the gate had grown a metre tall since the time he had left. Even though his friends had offered to drop him first, Bikash insisted on dropping them first. '*How very chivalrous of me to put myself in a tight spot,*' he thought to himself. Epiphanies of miscalculations buzzed around his head. Things only look and sound easy when one is intoxicated or in love, not knowing the difference between the two.

Once Bikash, drunk and furious, accepted random friend requests on Facebook, only to sit for hours and unfriend them after a night of heated argument with his girlfriend. Climbing the gate halfway, with one leg on each side, he suddenly felt wobbly. The gate swung to and fro, and for an instant, his entire life flashed before his eyes that led him to this situation, meanwhile trying to stabilise the gate.

Ironically, he could relate to all the alcoholics who sleep on the footpath and considered joining them just for the night. The entire idea of sleeping on the street seemed more comfortable than falling on his face and going another round with a fractured limb, leading to a major pay cut.

Ultimately, with great pondering atop the gate, he managed to slip his other leg through. Thanks to having watched enough Jackie Chan movies to overcome this hurdle, he gauged his distance and finally made the jump. Sadly, his trouser was pinched between the gate, causing it to tear from hip to thigh, which in turn led him to fall face down, striking his elbow on the stairs. Cold and pain don't go well; he lay there for a while, breathless, in excruciating pain. His alcohol had worn off, and when he got back to his room, he realised he had hit his knee as well. He quietly limped back to his room, not knowing what to hold, and passed out after getting into his cosy bed. Bikash slept like a baby that night.

SIREN

At the peak of every dusk and dawn, a shrill sound rises and falls in one corner of Darjeeling hill, either to wake them up or to put them down, echoing from hill to hill, screaming out loud. A siren horn goes off in the tea estate of the hills, echoing into the valley like ripples of water, breaking the mundane stillness.

As the starry drape of abyss began to fade, with each second black turned into pale blue and shades of red, the light gradually began to open its eyes, accompanied by a low hum, the musing sound of a pellucid river with its visceral eternal song of farewell that flows downhill with all the rich sediments.

Humble folks of Chongtong wake up before the sun and prepare their *fika-cheya*, a brew culminated from their hand-plucked and homemade leftover tea leaves that are often intentionally left down in their personal *doko*. If the "*Manager baw*" asks, they simply reply with a dissimulating smile, "*Oh, they got stuck again, sorry my doko is old!*" The base leaves are the ones to get plucked first and leave the basket last.

They generally begin their day with a light meal, a gentle smile blooming on their visage as they take a sneak peek into the cauldron, only to find the leftover rice that is perfectly paired with their sweetened black tea. From all the huts and cottages, a dim yellow light can be seen at approximately four, as some prepare to collect grass for their cattle, some to cook, and some to study for school. But Anuj's hut opens at five, along with the siren, neither before nor after it, and today was no exception.

Anuj rubbed his eyes, stretched and yawned, and ate the leftover rice with cold tea, left for him to savour by his one and only grandmother, who still wore an age-old, corroded gold nose *phuli*. When questioned about her most treasured jewel (phuli), her pale, wrinkled cheeks would reflect a mild tint of a perfectly brewed red tea. She would always gaze towards heaven and lose herself in distant reverie, vibrant, youthful days and would tell Anuj tales of her youth.

In one of her rough estimations, when inquired by Anuj about her birthday, today might be her probable day of birth, and it is celebrated by Anuj. She barely remembers where she last kept the sewing needle while holding it in her hand, hence her birthday falls amongst her least concerns. Every year since Anuj has started getting her a gift on this particular day, her peculiar demand has been constant: to witness Anuj get married.

Anuj manages to dodge the topic every time by muddling the whole notion into a joke. It was only a week ago that Anuj had discovered that his grandmother had never tasted chocolate cake, a brownie, or even a muffin. In fact, she was unaware of these sophisticated bakes. The closest thing to a dessert that she cherished was a bowl of kheer. She was a true minimalist, not by choice but by her decision to take care of Anuj in a crunched financial state. She made her living by plucking tea and had been surviving by doing so for the past thirty-five years. She was believed to be one of the most efficient workers, mostly because of her experience. However, she was only offered a handful of daily wages, Rs.137 and an additional bonus of Rs. 50 for which she would have to break her back.

Her juniors would often put up a sarcastic query, "*Boju, why wouldn't you rest, why do you work so hard?*" She would never frown and would simply reply;

"*I have a grandson; I have to prepare for his marriage.*"

The younger ladies would mumble under their breath, "*I wouldn't get married to his grandson until she is there.*" They would laugh and move on. Anuj's grandmother was aware of these nonsensical and mean comments but would never say a word in return. She was kind and yet remained aloof from such idiocracy. On the weekly "*Thursday haat,*" she had even paid the goldsmith for two simple engagement rings, which she held close to her bosom, wrapped in a cloth to save them from time and bad eyes.

Anuj, on the other hand, did not entertain any such words against his grandmother. He once knocked out a man twice his size because that man had called his grandmother a witch. Such absurdities are common in the hills, even today. A woman who has a shrill voice, is independent, and has no concern with society or the world at large is generally considered a witch, as they can sustain their needs, which the patriarchy does not allow.

Anuj had requested leave and was heading towards town for some special arrangements while his grandmother had already left for her work. He made chapati from the previous day's dough and took the *"bhutey ko mula ko saag,"* rolled it inside the chapati, and added it to his sling bag, in which he always kept his catapult and marbles, his favourite play tool as a kid and a faithful friend at work as a tea garden watchman. He carefully pulled out a bundle of hundreds from his cornermost coat, his annual secretive savings from his pocket money. Putting a few hundred rupee bills in his shirt pocket, he swung his sling bag and headed towards the five-foot-tall main door and into the open wide world.

The day seemed hopefully bright with momentary swirly, satin-like clouds in a cerulean sky and an aromatic breeze with a gentle scent of fresh April. A green canvas with momentary punctuations of velvety soft yet deep claret native flowers, Guras. To complement the harmonisation of nature, songs of flowing rivers echo through the valley.

Anuj sat in the local taxi, which he had booked a day prior. Birey Daju, the village's most flamboyant cab driver, would honk several times before he started his cab and mostly play popular songs by Manila and Udai Sotangs. His all-time favourite was *"Ukkali charawla, orali jharawla,"* a song about struggle, hardships, and determination of two lovers. Although his voice would not support his overflowing emotions, Birey Daju would sing at the top of his lungs. He would also entertain his passengers by sharing his tales of valour during his twenty-eight years of service in the army. Anuj would fancy his stories, for he loved the national army, but his love for the army could not compete with his love for his grandmother.

Somewhere amidst the loud song and Birey Daju's stories, someone asked, *"What time would you return today, Birey Daju?"* with a gentle but high-pitched voice.

"Probably by two, they have political demonstrations under the command of our great leaders!"

"No wonder so many trucks loaded with people headed towards the city today..."

Birey Daju mentioned the loaded trucks as if referring to sand or rocks piled up together to be used, something that is cheaply bought and sold, rather some inanimate objects which do not have any value of their own.

"Well, we are simple people, but this time Gorkhaland looks possible..."

Most of them agreed; some did not to Birey Daju's possibly half-semi-wise, semi-naive statement. The loud chatters fell silent, and only the melody remained:

"Gorkhali ko choro ho mo...

Gorkhe mero nam!"

High hopes, bright days, and an upbeat song by Mantra band, enough to make you sing along...

The taxi climbed, gravel and red soil-filled, verboten, inclined twists and turns, barely recognisable as roads. Roads in the hills are only fixed every three to five years. The same goes for clenched bonuses and promotions. The roads resemble the hollow speeches of renowned politicians. They erode with the same pace that they are fixed, the only difference between the latter and the former is of kind. Roads erode with seasonal rain and the first summer's sun.

The fake promises made in speeches fade with the passing season of election. Yet the people sleep with their eyes open, sleep as they are robbed of their rights. No one knows who or what cast this curse of eternal slumber, or when this nightmare will end? Would it be too late? Will they ever arise and see? For now, chicken rice and broken roads seem fine. We live today, now, but are we okay? Anuj thought to himself.

Before he knew it, the vehicle had already reached Darjeeling. The city, once in harmony with the beguiling Forest of Burchill, its mysticism, a town filled with joyful laughter, hopes and real dreams, now has become a cold, concrete place, both in essence and physical manifestation.

Surrounded by the hills and five treasures of the snow, a city where all hearts were gradually beginning to turn into concrete, just like the tall and suffocating buildings that had been constructed, calling it home. A shallow mask of joy promising divinity and a breathtaking nature, but underneath a rotting system, complaining, underpaid, poker-faced staff at hotels, shops, and restaurants, who are expected to work with their heart and soul. But the puppets do not have a soul, do they? They are mere tools of a ventriloquist.

In the background, traffic jams, carbon emissions, honks, and angry drivers trying to make more money result in poisoned nature that degrades in health every day. No traces of joy. No one had time to listen to the songs of Gainey and the melody of their sarangi. The crowd in Darjeeling is denser today, so are the honks and heads that wander aimlessly, and most of the shops are closed. Some goons had forcefully demanded to shut the shops, and most had closed their heart and shops due to the outstanding turmoil.

After picking up a card from his friend's studio, Anuj made his way to the old supermarket, crossing a good old bakery, Ghurramia. A bakery out of time, ignored and forgotten, a place at a standstill after its glorious days. *"So I will have to go a little out of budget..."* Anuj thought to himself. Moving against the waves of people that came from opposite directions to attend the demonstration against the language imposition initiated by the state government. Anuj was unaware of this. For him and many others like him, our *"brave leaders"* were fighting to bring back the lost glory of the land, but he could not openly support them as his grandmother hated politics for some reason, and to him, his grandmother's words were final. The agitation was even termed the *"Gorkhaland movement!"*

Despite this emotional and ideological tug of war, Anuj's only concern was his grandmother's birthday cake. He finally reached Walis after battling against the wave of humans that flowed downwards to the designated area of mass gathering. Anuj went under the half-lifted shutter of the shop.

"How much for the cake?"

"350/- for one pound, but that one was pre-ordered. We don't have any for sale. We can prepare it tomorrow, daju."

"Can I pay fifty rupees more for the cake? It is an important day today, and you have just the right flavour. It's a humble request."

"I understand, daju. I wish I could help, but I can't sell it. That cake has been requested by our regular customer."

"You could take the black forest pastry instead. It is closer…"

Someone from outside kicked the shutter and screamed with a heavy voice. *"Close your shutter, you ungrateful fool! We are letting you stay at our place, and yet you dare to defy us?"*

The shopkeeper hurriedly packed the pastries in a box and pushed it towards Anuj. *"Daju, please leave. We cannot sell you the cake, and we do not want any trouble."*

"How much do I owe you for these?"

"They are on the house, daju. Now please leave. We are really sorry."

"Chotu, close the shutter!"

Anuj was pushed out of the shop. The chaos outside had settled, and the quietness was almost disturbing. Only the pack of stray dogs remained, as though humanity was wiped out from the face of the earth along with their problems. No sign of a crowd and the goons who were beating the doors and shutters of half-closed shops had left.

Anuj stretched his left arm and wiped the face of his watch to read the time—his grandfather's watch handed down to him along with the mannerism. Worn-out leather strap and rust compiled next to the crown, the only new-looking part of the watch was its glass case. The watch held onto his wrist somehow. As he walked his way to the taxi syndicate, he could see a few people still heading down towards Singamari. Birey Daju had parked his vehicle next to the old supermarket due to parking constraints caused by the procession. Anuj opened the back seat door and entered.

"That was quick of you. Are you done with all your work?"

"Yes, Birey Daju, I did not have much work today…"

"Did you have your lunch?"

"Not yet, daju. How about you?"

"Come, let's go. Lunch is on me."

"You are too kind, daju, but I've brought my own food."

"It's okay. You don't have to be shy. Come and drink some tea at least."

They still had time. It was thirty past one, and there was ample time to eat and prepare for the return. Only a few weeks back, the C.R.P.F. and the army jawans were offered meals and beverages by the picketers. There were no signs of violence. Even the demonstrations were peaceful, and the state government was docile.

They found Nitesh gulping down 'raksi' at the small restaurant where they had gone to eat. Nitesh had a badly done snake tattoo on his forearm, and he always wore a leather jacket, irrespective of the weather condition. A short but healthy-looking man, with dreadlocks in his hair, yellow eyes due to alcohol consumption, he was often armed with a khukuri. A local goon.

Nitesh had two kids and a young wife. He was an abusive man. He would come home drunk and beat his children and wife and was even jailed for robbery once. A notorious individual and now one of the members of the leading party. Anuj and Nitesh had been childhood friends, but they rarely spoke to each other in recent times. As soon as Nitesh saw Anuj, he rested his glass and tried to act sober.

Nitesh: "*Anuj, my friend, my brother, how have you been?*"

Anuj: "*Good, and you?*"

Nitesh: "*I've never been great. Following our great leader was the best decision of my life. We will get our motherland this time, we shall succeed, and as said by our leader, the future of our children will be good!*"

Anuj: "*I, too, believe so, my friend.*"

Nitesh: "*I was always the bad one, making trouble, but you were good at studying. You could have become a schoolmaster with ease. Why did you choose this life? When we get our land, please do something that you are capable of, okay?*"

Nitesh placed his naked blade on the table and gave an atrocious smile. Birey Daju watched in silent horror, and Nitesh's friends became quiet. The external void poured into the room through the ajar limestone-painted door. Anuj cleared his throat. Meanwhile, the lid of moktu was dropped by the restaurant owner, and that's when Nitesh picked up his khukuri and added to the sound.

"Let's go, boys…"

The uneasiness gradually lifted, and Birey Daju hit the nail on the coffin by saying, *"I've long given up on violence. Otherwise, I would have copped him like a radish."*

Giggles of the shopkeeper lady could be heard till outside. Birey angrily asked for two cups of tea. He told Anuj to keep away from such people and mind his own business. Whatever happened left a long-lasting impression on Anuj's mind, and he contemplated what Nitesh could have meant with whatever he had just said. Not that they were best friends, that Nitesh would be concerned with Anuj's well-being. Besides, the last time they had spoken on good terms was seven years back when they had bunked school together, and Anuj received a nice beating from his grandmother. He was forbidden to keep any relation with Nitesh.

Anuj took out the chapati and offered it to Birey Daju, which he politely declined and said that they had to leave as soon as it was almost two. All the passengers had gathered in the vehicle and were ready. Anuj could only take a bite of the chapati and a few sips of his tea when other passengers began to panic. Birey Daju completed his honking ritual and moved his vehicle towards their destination. The roads were pretty much empty until they reached near the Singamari police station, where the demonstrators had surrounded the station and were shouting slogans of;

"We want justice, we want Gorkhaland!"

The traffic would not clear soon. Hence, Birey Daju began to turn the vehicle towards Darjeeling again. The route would be longer. However, it would be better than having a broken windshield. As he grumpily mumbled and turned the vehicle, two gunshots rippled in the air, disrupting the stillness of the traffic jam, and the chaos broke out like a can of tinned beans falling on the floor. There were screams of men and women, a stampede, and a few still trying to retaliate. A lady ran screaming, *"They shot someone, they shot someone." Birey Daju panicked even more after hearing this, and everyone in the car started to scream at him.*

Meanwhile, Anuj could not feel anything, could not hear anything, as though the shots were fired next to his ears. He froze and could not think straight. His thoughts vaporised. The voices, screams, everything! Sweaty palms, short breaths, cold air. He looked at his numb palms and gathered his courage to look outside. The men in uniform were beating someone to a pulp, a road stained with an individual's blood. Beside him lay a lifeless body.

Anuj opened the door and rushed towards the scene, his hands automatically reaching for his sling bag. He shot a man in uniform with his catapult, creating confusion. He dragged the lifeless body and tried to reach the vehicle, but it was nowhere to be seen. He then tried to run as fast as his legs would allow him. He heard a loud bang and felt a crippling pain in his right posterior thigh, making him lose his balance as he fell face down with the body on top of him. The sound of approaching boots haunted him. His arms again reached for his sling bag, but before he could take it out, he saw a boot approaching his face, making him momentarily lose his consciousness. He blinked his eyes and tried to clear his blurred vision. Due to the excessive bleeding from his head, he could no longer feel his arms, and a few of his teeth were loose. As he tried to shake this off and rise, a final blow was delivered to the back of his head with a rifle's butt, rendering him unconscious and sending him to the unknown, eternal abyss.

The chaos continued. Police and C.R.P.F. began their relentless raids. According to police reports, the violence was initiated by the mob, as one of the absconded individuals tried to forcefully break through the barricade. The eyewitnesses from the political party stated that the men in uniform instigated violence by ordering a lathi charge on the mob that was peacefully demonstrating.

The news was sold, some real, some fake. Everyone had their own story to tell. No one knew what had happened that afternoon except the fact that three lives were claimed. A vintage blood-stained watch was found at the site of the incident.

On the evening of the incident, Birey Daju's vehicle reached its destination at 16:48. The siren rang shortly after with its deafening effects. Only the shapeless black forest pastry reached Anuj's home, and the river sang the eternal song of farewell.

Three days later, a blood-stained identical bag to Anuj's came looking for his grandmother's home. She had already demanded to see her grandson but was denied, stating that Anuj was critical. The bag contained the postmortem reports, his favourite catapult made by his grandfather, a few marbles, a half-eaten chapati, and a sample wedding card that read...

Anuj weds Naina.

INTERVIEW

‘BEEP-BEEP, BEEP-BEEP’

"It's already morning? I thought I slept only a while ago!"

"Anita, wake up. It's the second time that thing has rung. You'll be late…"

It had been a decade since she had heard that nurturing voice, a voice that cared and was stern just the right amount. But now she had a life of her own, and Anita was left all alone in the vastness of eternity. Somewhere in her new apartment in Safdarjung, Delhi, she was now a cabin supervisor for a reputed airline. She recalled the challenges of the interview day and smiled as she prepared for her flight. The same alarm rang every morning, evening, night, and afternoon. No particular demarcation of the day could be concluded if the roster said it was time to wake up and leave for a flight.

The similar sound of the alarm had violently woken her up a few years back for the interview. She distinctly remembered the wind blowing past the grills, pushing in the white curtains. A messy bed, still warm, undone laundry in the laundry bag, and a jumping electric kettle ready to spill out, a mug with a spoon full of coffee. A fan spun lethargically, but it still went in circles, creaking and squeaking as though it had accepted its fate.

Anita went in front of the mirror and practised her replies for the probable interview questions while brushing her teeth. She revised the lines several times while the thin bristles rubbed against her teeth, mentally reviewing. She then giggled as the vision of her proudly walking out of the interview door after being selected struck her mind. She jumped in excitement, washed her face, hurriedly stirred the coffee, and dabbed her face with a towel. Pulling out the makeup box, she took a sip of the coffee and shrieked, making an agonising face. She did not enjoy coffee, but working late nights at the BPO company to climb the ladder had made her almost addicted to it. Tea used to be her thing.

If Anita had decided to stay with the BPO, she would have been promoted to a full manager, with her own cabin and a handsome salary raise. But the position was unjustly offered to her junior, as they were related to higher management. Besides, Anita had a family to look after. She was the sole breadwinner of the family. She had been working for the past four years, right after college, yet she struggled to pay her bills and always had to borrow from her friends by the end of the month.

Anita put on her black and white business attire. This would be the last day of her wearing these old formals. She would have several new ones once she landed her new job. Anita took her document folder, took a deep breath, gently pulled the door behind her, and exited towards the windy day. Her mental review never ended, although she was momentarily disturbed by secondary thoughts of her mother's ill health and her sister's abusive husband and how she would take them away from this place and keep them with her, just like the good old days, when stomachs might be half-empty, but they were always together.

Meanwhile, the gust had brought travellers from the far distant wilderness of the sea. A grey ink-blotted canvas set behind her, and the day looked gloomier as she boarded the rusty foothold of the rickshaw. She carefully sat down so as not to crumple her neatly ironed formals. Mild, cool wind gently brushed her face and other exposed parts of her skin. She could not complain, as she could not afford to be late and had already wasted valuable moments bargaining with the rickshaw puller. She hurriedly handed him the twenty-rupee note they had agreed upon and ran towards the bus stand. The bus to Bagdogra had just stopped.

A bus that would lead her to her dreams and elevate her to a better lifestyle. Her mother had taken her to the village shaman, who had observed the white rice grains with immense care and curiosity as though his life depended on it. As a matter of fact, his life did depend on it. He was one of the most renowned shamans in the Salbari area. He would roll his eyes and chant outlandish incantations, then blow a few times into his closed palm, only to show his spectators the changed colour of the rice when he opened his palm. All these tricks made him popular amongst the local folks, who would only read the horoscope page in the weekly telegram and wait for the daily horoscope in the morning news channels. It is normal for people to become inclined towards such beliefs. It's rather the 'herd mentality' that percolates into one's psyche.

Although Anita was a well-educated individual and had worked with Pan-Indian cultures, she still believed in the supernatural, must have been her upbringing. 'Sante-Guruji' had pointed out that Anita would definitely secure the job if she worshipped her version of God. She even read a highly positive feedback from the horoscope. It was as though all things nudged towards success; nothing could take her down, as she believed. Bold, proactive, and well-prepared. That is what she was today; that is how she felt. However, a constant fear kept on ringing at the back of her head and her shoulders were stiff. Meanwhile, the clouds seemed darker as Anita boarded the bus and looked outside the window. The nimbus roared with unbearable weight, and with the thunderclap began the first spell of rain.

Anita began the reruns of the questions she had prepared, over and over and over again, like a stuck gramophone. If she spoke her thoughts out loud, it would be absurd to observe her. By the time she reached the venue, the drizzle had transformed into rain. Rain has a healing and cleansing effect; it washes away impurities and offers new life and freshness to the tired old trees that patiently wait.

She clumsily ran towards the waiting hall with a file on top of her head, struggling to keep her tote on her shoulder. She then took a deep breath, adjusted her clothes one last time, straightened her back, dropped her shoulders, and practised her smile, faking it from one molar to the other. She wished the guard, receptionist, and everyone else in the vicinity. She wore a mask in order to be accepted in a world of masks. She wished the girl who looked nervous;

"Good morning, I'm Anita. You look nervous. Are you okay? Do you want some water to drink?"

The girl returned a smile filled with trepidation, "Hello, I'm Sruti. No, thank you."

"Are you sure? You look worried. Is it your first time?"

"Yes, and I think I forgot my High School certificate."

"Don't worry. They will only check your CV today."

"Oh, that's a relief. Thank you."

The interviewers came in half an hour late. The empty hall now looked like the Hong Kong market on a busy Sunday, chatters and small talk everywhere, fake smiles, hollow concerns, some were even exchanging numbers, which they would definitely lose after the interview. These people believed they were prepared after consuming the same *"Tricks to Becoming a Cabin Crew"* videos/articles. Perhaps, the lost sense of deluded individuality can be most highlighted in interviews as such, where everyone wants to look and be different, but with the identical set of notions.

Anita had been through enough interviews to know the difference. Hence, she had prepared differently. Even though she had been wearing the same old black and white business suit almost all her life, she had bought a brand new blue silk scarf from her personal allowance. She wore a rose knot and had done smoky eye shades with blue, with light blushers that made her look very bold and appealing, not to mention her fair skin tone that made everything look perfectly in place.

She was amongst the first hundred to show up for the interview. The initial interviews were longer and lasted 3-5 minutes, but as the day went by, it seemed the panel's patience was wearing thin. By the time it hit token number 45, the interview time had grown shorter, lasting only a minute and a half. By this time, the waiting hall had settled down to mere whispers, and the freshness of the flowery perfumes had now wilted and started to mix with the stench of sweat and warm breaths. The air conditioning worked just fine, but most of them felt hot, and a few shivered in cold sweat.

Anita wiped her palms several times. She wished she could wash her face, but the makeup that took her hours would wash off in seconds. She confined herself to just dabbing her face with the facial tissue several times. While others swarmed around the interviewees who exited the room, Anita stood her ground. It could have been her pride, or maybe her reserved nature, that she had developed over the years of repealing unwanted attention from men. She sat there in her seat, ready to be called upon next. The interviewer came outside and announced a break for thirty minutes.

A wave of disappointed chatter splashed in the room as everyone started to leave for the tea break. Endless clicking of high heels and the aroma of tea filled the room.

Not many people were left in the hall; even her nervous companion had gone, but she remained unmoved. Anita sat in utmost silence with just her thoughts and a room full of empty chairs, as all the noise had now been transferred to another hall. Shortly, the interviewers came out and smiled at Anita, and one was even kind enough to ask if she was okay. To which Anita replied with a polite,

"Yes, ma'am, and thank you for your concern."

Anita built her focus and began her mental review again, but this time, her mind seemed to drift elsewhere. She remembered the faces of her mother, sister, and even the friend who

had recently passed away. She drifted away from there. Hence, she was there, yet she was not. Her eyes welled, and she could barely see the room. She hurriedly dabbed her eyes with a tissue and ran towards the bathroom to fix her makeup. She began to pant wildly and shiver, and she could not help but think, why here and now, of all places, and why today?

As she sat shaking on the toilet seat in that three-by-one ply wall, she heard two voices entering the washroom, and they rushed out, stating it was almost time. This further sent Anita into a state of breathlessness and turmoil. She gathered the courage and strength to collect herself and dashed towards the mirror. Luckily, her makeup was still intact, but her palpating heart said otherwise, and her stomach turning upside down did not help her either. She conducted a light touch-up with her shaky hands, took a couple of deep breaths, and practised her smile a couple of times before leaving the washroom.

Anita opened the door and smiled at the three awkwardly arranged faces stopped from falling apart by the makeup.

"May I come in, ma'am?"

Anita sought permission to sit. One of the interviewers was not done with her donut and coffee, and Anita was gestured to wait as she waited helplessly. Still with her shaky voice and a timid smile, all her confidence had melted away, her mental review wiped clean, like a classroom green board on a weekend.

A green board has nothing to offer except creativity and imagination. Provided it is placed in the right place, a clean green board would be better suited to a lunatic asylum or a kids' room. The power to see, imagine, and admire art fades away with age and so-called sanity. Anita's mind had somehow become the very green board, blank.

She smiled nervously while standing with her large file in front of her. Her heels had, by this time, started biting into her feet, and her sole felt as though someone had been trying to insert a nail into it with utmost care and precision. In this pain, she felt like her feet were confined in the heels.

The panellist with the donut was finally done. She gestured to Anita to proceed further and sit. Anita moved towards the chair as steadily as she could and barely made it to the chair before her leg gave up and she stumbled. Her breakdown did not make it easier on her. She began to shake, and only an awkward smile could be forced out. Ultimately, one of the interviewers, the gentler by appearance, broke the discomfort of the silence with,

"*Are we not done yet?*"

With a tilted head, as if to say, "*We need to finish this, and there is someone looking at us*" or even, "*Could you stop already?*" Then the donut lady shot a question at Anita, with mean eyes and penetrating looks.

"*So why do you want to join our company?*"

This question sent a chilly smile down her spine, and she could feel the floor slip beneath her feet. She froze and could not recall a single thing she had been practising for so long. She knew the number of destinations, the date the company started, the yearly turnover of the company, the number of destinations they were to add, the number of customers retained. In fact, too many numbers. All that flashed in front of her were just numbers, unclear numbers. It is sad how sometimes knowing more fails us in life rather than not knowing. "*Would a fool's paradise be a real three-dimensional space?*" where all is but joy and easygoing. As knowing is a burden in itself, would not knowing that one truly does not know anything also be a burden?

By the time Anita resurfaced from her delusion, the interview was already over. She had surprisingly given all the answers, and the interviewers fancied her reply as well. She would finally occupy her dream job, and her training would resume in a few weeks. She rushed out of the waiting hall area and then jumped, her ailing heels all but a thing of the past.

Today.

She had her breakfast and prepared for her flight while listening to "*The Great Pretender*" by the Platters. She checked her roster. As a lead, she mostly did domestic sectors, but she never complained about her work. There was not much room to. She mostly operated with her four basic set of crew, limited customers, and no complaints. She even knew some of them. Mr. Paul was a frequent flier and always motivated her to do more and better. He even offered her mints and sweets every now and then, and those candies were indeed "*magical*" as Mr. Paul would remark.

Anita had finally made it, but at times, she would feel sick, and every time she felt sick, the piano chords would ring off notes in those songs, or the walls would look disturbingly dirty, and even when the witch-doctor would start to whisper words that she did not understand in her ears, turning her almost deaf. All she had to do was pop a blue candy offered by Mr. Paul, and it would all go away.

BALLOON MAN

Tristan sat in the cab that he had called ten minutes ago, parking his bag beside him with one hand while holding an envelope in the other. His bag was oddly oversized for the front seat, and the driver did not seem very polite. He was rather a simple old man with a frail frame and a grumpy mug. On the contrary, Tristan was on the opposite spectrum of age, still exploring the possibilities that the world threw at him in bits and pieces.

A soft-spoken, fairly neat, and pale-complexioned young man, Tristan had a decent height back in his hometown, Kalimpong. He had typical Lepcha eyes and a smile that could brighten anyone's day. Although he always kept to himself, he was a natural empath. However, he was decisively quiet today. He neither felt the need to understand his driver's grumpiness nor to explain the abnormality of his bag. His interest in the office had also been dwindling with each passing day.

The driver turned around with a certain jerk, scratching his whiskers, to snoop something, but Tristan had long transcended his present, flying somewhere in volume 4 of Archduke Trio, away from all the hustle and bustle of fast-paced life, aloof from time. He had wafted into the rebellious, uncanny notes of Beethoven, which spilt all his bottled-up feelings. The Uber driver, now scratching his head, turned back around and twisted the key. They made it to the flyover in no time. The driver seemed pretty experienced as he drove without rushing, and his gear shifting was smooth. He followed the traffic lights, a rare sight in Bombay.

They stopped near the railway station. On the left side of the taxi were the footpaths and high fences, beyond which were the railway tracks. Tristan observed the silent trains that almost seemed hollow as they passed by, similar to things that come and slip from our hands in the span of time. The whole phenomenon barely made sense. If you are playful and susceptible to change, you'll often find yourself smiling just as Tristan did.

His daylight reverie broke when he was drawn towards the drowning yellow orb, which left the sky blushing with its warm tones of pink, red, and yellow. A 'pao'-sized fist, merely dangling from a limb that could be mistaken for a stick, knocked at his window. Outside stood a lean girl in a shabby, loosely fitted yellow frock with blue, red, and green polka dots. Her black irises on a cream-white backdrop in concave eye sockets, filled with void yet hope, desire, and agony, contrasted with a warm and genuine smile. A smile that even the proud sun would have to acknowledge. How could he resist? Tristan was a mere human, after all. She held balloons of different shades in her other hand, floating and dancing with a mild, soft breeze that blew time and again. Tristan slowly rolled down the window and smiled;

"Hello, little miss, how may I help you?"

"Sir, please buy some balloons. I haven't eaten, and I have a little brother to feed."

Pointing at the half-bare child, leaning backwards on the fence, who wore a banyan and seemed frazzled by carrying the weight of his own oversized head, Tristan began to fish the front pocket of his bag. With a quick struggle, he took out packets of almonds and melted chocolates and handed them to her.

"These are for you and your brother."

Her eyes twinkled with joy. It was as though the eclipse had disappeared, and light had unveiled itself over her, even if just for that instant. Tristan felt a little ticklish sensation of joy in his heart as though he had just received those gifts from a stranger. A gloom soon fogged up her visage, making it go dull and pale again. At this moment, Tristan realised an uncanny discomfort for the balloon not being sold. He understood she would have to be answerable later in the evening. Without a second thought, he drew his wallet out and asked,

"Well then, how much for the balloon?"

Her face lit up again, and she replied with a sudden jerk and a smile of similar intensity, "Rs. *30!*" More with her eyes, almost breaking into a joyful scream.

"But I don't have any change on me, do you?"

She sadly shook her head, sinking in withdrawal and looking at her bare blistered feet. The driver turned behind, with his hand in his mustard shirt's pocket, with a mild trace of a smirk. Tristan, however, had made up his mind by now.

"How many do you have?"

She looked up and counted while pulling in her snot and keeping a keen track of the count on her fingers, adroit in daily work. However, today she had her eyes on the blue one that she fancied and wished it wouldn't get sold. She was hesitant to sell it but finally making up her mind, she replied with a heavy heart and a discontinued smile.

It is funny how life sets us in contradictory situations. She almost cried while she placed her tightly clenched fist forward and said, *"I have fifteen balloons."*

He took a Rs. 500 note from his wallet and smiled with his eyes, as though making sure she knew what to do next. He entrusted her with that piece of paper and said:

"You may keep the change and keep this one for yourself and your brother."

Tristan handed her the blue and yellow balloon and held the rest tightly. He smiled like a little boy, making sure he did not let go this time. By now, the traffic had cleared. He seemed amused by the whole idea of holding thirteen balloons. It was surely a lot for a thirty-one-year-old bachelor, but those gas-filled rubbers had always been his favourite plaything, even as a kid. Time and again, he looked in the direction of the balloons and smiled in genuine admiration as he rested his cheeks on his elbow on the window.

He was taken aback by a wild jolt. He pulled himself inside and tried to inspect his driver in the front seat. The driver looked unconscious. Tristan tried to wake him up, but he seemed to have collapsed, with his head down on the steering wheel, honking all the way like an express train. Before Tristan could make a move, a speeding army truck rammed their vehicle. The glasses on the opposite door began to crack, each crack branching out and replicating itself multiple times until it finally shattered and the pieces went flying in all directions. His heart raced, almost pummelling on his ribcage. His driver, still unconscious, just moved left to right on the wheel. The 4.5-tonne monster kept pressing them towards the wall until they finally hit a barricade, sending the vehicle flying three feet off the ground. The vehicle rolled multiple times until it finally stopped close to the flyover wall.

Despite his head being slammed multiple times on the interior, Tristan remained conscious. He looked at his hands, still holding those balloons, although he could barely feel his hand. He tried to shake the driver with his bloody hands, but he seemed sound asleep. Tristan's bloodshot eyes could no longer make clear distinctions. The last thing he noticed was his femur had managed to tear through his flesh and the jeans he wore, now no longer clean and soaked with his own blood. He thought to himself, "*Ama would be really mad and upset if she saw these dirty jeans,*" a fairly spontaneous thought at an unsolicited time. Dark shadows and shapes slowly blanketed him. It seemed to be getting colder, but he felt warm somehow as he slowly slid into the abyss.

He blinked his eyes multiple times in disbelief. His legs were dangling from the iron rail of the third-floor balcony. They were small, a mere size one. He observed the few kids playing on the playground and scanned through the tall buildings that looked lifeless and hollow. This was him, it was him from many years back! Why would this memory reach him now? He wondered but did not give it much thought.

Tristan was bored and had nothing much to do. His only friend Nannu had gone for the puja vacation, but they couldn't afford it as they lived far away, and the train was the only means of transport. He had tied a string on a plastic bag, which he pretended to be a kite. The blue polythene gracefully danced every time the wind blew past his balcony. He wished he could do the same. He enacted the dogs and barked at them in hopes he could be acquainted with them and play with their puppies. Meanwhile, ants crawled near him, but he did not want to feed them again. His mama would get suspicious if he went into the kitchen twice.

It was at this moment that he saw a lean and tall man at a distance, walking with a cycle equipped with a cylinder and a box attached to its backseat. The bicycle's handle was decorated with colourful bags and floating balloons tied to strings of all colours. He definitely had a lot of them. All the kids ran down to him, even those playing in the park.

Tristan leaned back 90°, holding the rails. His mum was still busy cooking, wearing a nightie. It surely looked melting hot in there, and his ama often seemed in her worst mood when in the kitchen. Tristan gathered all the courage he could, gulped the saliva he was playing with in his mouth a little while ago, and said, "*Ama…*"

Without paying much attention to him, she was still waiting for the curry to turn perfectly brown. No reply from her, guessing she might not have heard him. "*Aa… mmmaaa…*" (slightly louder than before)

"*What is it? Tristan, I hear you. Can't you see I'm doing something out here? If you need anything, come here and tell me!*"

Tristan slowly pulled his dangling legs up and held the walls behind him, he looked at his feet and walked towards the kitchen, clearing his throat he said.

"Ama, there is a balloon man, next to the park."

"What should I do about it, Tristan?"

"I was thinking if I could get one…please."

"Not now, I'm busy waiting for your father to come and he will take you."

"I can go and get it myself."

His ama turned and gave him a short stare, a clear signal that she did not wish to be bothered any further. Tristan looked at his feet and walked back to his previous spot. He carefully placed his legs where they originally were and rested his face on the iron rail. Half of the balloons were gone by this time, and the kids, with warm and happy faces, walked away with their parents, holding a balloon in one hand and a firm, nurturing hand in the other.

His patience knew no bounds today. He shook his legs and watched as the balloons disappeared one after the other. He softly tapped the iron rail with his little fingers, then looked at the watch back and forth; it read 01:55. No matter how many times he did this, the time wouldn't change. There were still five minutes left before his father came back from the office.

The balloon man rang the red bell mounted on the handle of his bicycle. He rang it twice, ending with a shrill ping, alerting the commuters that it was his time to leave. Tristan's eyes welled up with cold tears; he really loved balloons, after all. They were light and came in different colours and shapes. Especially the ones filled with the magic gas from the tank—they would float as far as his little eyes could chase them. He now began to swing his legs even faster, grasping the iron rail and shaking to and fro.

He looked back at the watch: 01:57. Three more minutes to go. He wanted to appeal to his ama, but he couldn't let the balloon man vanish from his sight. Moreover, he knew he would surely be made to understand with her slipper that she did not have time for his foolish plea. Holding back his shaky voice and tears, he gulped down the little saliva he had collected. He gasped for more air, but his tiny lungs could only take in what was necessary to function. The balloon man was stopped by an array of new kids, and Tristan's breathing became normal.

Then he heard the doorbell ring twice, just the way his father did, two short bursts. He hurriedly pulled his legs up and rushed towards the door, pulling a plastic chair from the dining table and unlatching the door with all the effort his tiny hands could muster. Pushing back the chair, he opened the heavy quarter door. It always felt like opening a tank door. He jumped at his father's legs and started weeping while tapping his feet. His father, although irritated from work, held Tristan in his muscular arms and inquired;

"Ama? Did you give him some pasting?"

"No, he just wanted a balloon, and I was busy with my chores."

His father looked at him and smiled, *"So my champion was crying for a balloon, was it?"*

Tristan, already in tears, nodded his head in agreement. There was a sense of rush but an ironic calm that everything would be alright. His father was the strongest. He would do push-ups with Tristan on his back and rode faster than the milkman's bike. He was the best! They both climbed down the staircase, Tristan holding his father's huge hands, his father towering over him. They both sat on his father's bicycle and rode to glory.

Luckily, the balloon man was still surrounded by more kids. Tristan smiled at his father with tears in his eyes, and his father smiled back at him. They finally made it to the balloon man. Tristan chose a huge yellow balloon and looked at the quarter where they stayed. It looked like a small zoo, with a white background and black-painted iron rails. His father inquired, *"Tristan, are we happy now?"*

Tristan nodded his head up and down with a big smile. They both sat on the cycle again, Tristan on the tiny seat in front of his father, a seat especially customised for him. Tristan felt the route was shorter than before. He proudly held the balloon, admiring it. But an evil gust of wind blew and took his dear balloon away. He tried to jump and grab it by its thread, only to almost fall on his face if it weren't for his father's quick reflexes. His father now had an irritated look on his face; his rest period was getting hampered.

He quickly turned the bicycle and headed towards the balloon man before Tristan could utter a word. This time Tristan did not get to choose. His father picked a red balloon with random colourful dots on top. It did float in the air, though. His father hurried and began to tie the balloon to the cycle, but Tristan insisted on holding it.

His father asked him to hold it as tightly as he could. They both rode back again. As they were about to reach their building, another strong and evil gust of wind took Tristan's balloon away. He watched it until it turned into a mere black speck that vanished behind the tall and hollow buildings. He had an urge to cry but understood that his father was tired, so he quietly sat on the front seat with his eyes on the fast road that ran beneath them. Thick tears started to roll down. His father didn't say a word, and Tristan dared not ask him for another one.

They reached the building, and his father commanded him to go up as he locked his cycle. Tristan sluggishly climbed up the stairs with slouchy shoulders, dragging his feet with immense effort. One step at a time, his flip-flops seemed louder and heavier today. He finally reached the top and pushed the door open with both hands, quietly sitting where he had been before, placing his face between the black iron rails. His ama inquired about the balloon but did not get any answer, so she went back to her chores. The balloon man was no longer there. All that was left on the opposite side of the children's park were those expressionless tall and hollow buildings.

His father's footsteps approached him, but he did not look back. A blue balloon dangled in front of his face. He shifted his gaze from the balloon to his father and said thank you, but this balloon did not excite him. It dangled, such a stupid balloon. Why would it not fly like the others? His father smiled, replaced the previous polythene bag with the balloon, and went in to freshen up.

A gust of wind stroked his hair yet again, and the balloon touched his leg as though it wanted to play with Tristan. He no longer had the urge to play with the balloon. Without a second thought, he grabbed the string and snapped it with his frail teeth, watching the balloon as it danced away. Sadly, the balloon couldn't fly any further, as it was blown by his father's strong lungs and not the magic cylinder. It landed on the ripe, wheat-brown grass and met its fate. It burst open with a mild sound, air gushing out, and the rubber went in all directions.

Tristan opened his indolent eyes. A crowd of tall black shadows surrounded him. Slowly, the orange light filled in, and he was back to his suffering, back in the mundane city, gasping for air. Wheezing sounds came from his frail and paradoxical chest, blood oozing out from his mouth, choking him every once in a while as he exhaled heavily. His body was still numb with pain, and he still held on to the balloon with his numbed right hand. Few people fished for his pockets and took his belongings: wallet, phone, watch. Some took pictures; many made videos of his broken crown and dismantled leg. He could vaguely record all this with his fading conscience. Surprisingly, he held his blood-stained resignation letter in his left hand.

Tristan swallowed the saliva mixed with blood that ailed his dry throat while recalling all his family members, even those who had long left him. His loving grandparents and father. Wintery tears filled his eyes and slowly rolled down his blood-soaked face as he realised no one would be there to feed his sick younger sister and widowed Ama.

He tried to hold on to the balloons with all his might, but his fingers disregarded his command. They slipped from his grasp, one string at a time, from his blood-soaked palm. The balloons flew further and further away, as far as Tristan could see them. He raised his arms about a foot above the ground as if reaching out to grasp the strings. Fading images and faint sounds filled his mind. His lifeless arm fell on the street, and the eyes that once glittered with passion now lacked life. He lost sight of the balloons, only this time the cold and hollow buildings were replaced by hollow and cold humans. He sank just like that balloon punctured on the dry grass, with a faint sound, as the final ounce of air escaped his body. He left behind an ironically bright smile, as though to prove that his mother and sister would be okay even after he was gone.

Perhaps this was his most cherished memory.

BISCUIT

Time and again humans have tried to remember something intangible, something they can cherish and smile about, something they can recall at the most unexpected hour and place.

That particular something of no material value yet equally valuable in essence, something to remind them and offer them a resonance to one's existence, *Memento mori*.

As suggested by philosophers from time immemorial and by modern-day sociologists and anthropologists, celebrations are mere time markers of human existence to notify them of the remaining time one finds of value and demarcates as a part of recurrent existential experiences one transcends through their phases of life. In general, humans celebrate abiding by the rules of religion and rituals, but some do exist out of sheer will, only for the sake of being remembered.

We remember one such blip, an instance where humans have tried to overdo their existence and failed beautifully. This is a narrative of a sidereal day of an ordinary boy named Akash...

He woke up at six in the morning; his mother took him for a bath. It was too early for him, even if he wasn't too tired from all the playing with his friend Rupam next door. The place where Akash and his family lived was a slowly progressing housing complex for the new soldiers. All the flats were temporary and restricted to the ground floor. A minuscule developing village of Punjab, the locals often mingled with the army family as the area had not been barricaded. Aakash wondered why his mother forced him to wake up and made him brush his teeth as she filled the bucket from the hand-pump. Were they going to meet Grandpa and Grandma again? But they had only come back a few days back. So many things ran through his head as he chewed on his brush and swallowed the paste, sitting naked and waiting to be washed by his mother.

He had curly hair of a certain length, which his mother would part into two piggie-tails. He did not like his hair being parted and would always cry. Today he was quiet; he looked at his mother as she combed his hair and tied it with a rubber band.

"Ma…Ma…"

"What are we doing today?"

"Today is not my bath day. Are we going somewhere?"

"Yes, we are going to the Gurudwara, to pray to god."

Akash belongs to a religious family. He usually prays every night by clenching his eyes and joining his little hands in front of the poster of Shiv and Parvati. He prays for the well-being of his grandparents and parents and for some toys he could play with. A bit much for his age, but not too much as well. Usually, he wakes up around eight and waits for his father at the main gate with half a glass of milk held with both his hands.

His father would come only after eight fifteen from his night-long duty from the post. His father would approach the main gate from his night-long shift, on foot with his combat uniform, lethargically, clenching to the last ounce of his energy, but his face would glow up, it would reflect the scintillating hopes and aspirations of his son. He would lift up Akash and inquire about his dream. Akash would illustrate his beautiful dreams to his father with great enthusiasm, and his father would listen with equanimity, despite his eyes burdened with sleep and his shoulders burdened with responsibility. Solitude does change a man, not many are capable of harnessing it. Today, Akash could not wait for his father, as he was too early to receive his father, and they were going to the "Gu-ru-da-ra," as Akash would pronounce it, Gurudwara.

His mother applied white powder all over his body from below his neck and dressed him in his new shirt and pants, which were bought for him previous Dusherra and had been neatly folded and kept inside the big tin box. He dug his face in them and took a deep breath; it smelled of camphor. Camphor smelled good, he thought. He asked;

"Maa... why are we going to the Gu-ru-da-ra?"

"Because it is someone's birthday today!"

He suddenly sprung up from the bed with undone shoelaces and started dancing, "*Yae! It's my birthday! It's my birthday!*"

His mother smiled and put a black circle behind his left ear with kohl and said, "*Okay big boy, calm down and wait for Ama to get ready, okay?*"

He shook his head in agreement and waited on the chair kept right in front of the door. Akash wanted to tell how he had caught a big fish in his dream and how he was a pirate captain of a dangerous-looking blue ship, but he was distracted by a sparrow that had come and sat in the front yard, near the feed. It jumped around and chirped, but none of its friends came, so it flew away. Akash ran to the door and placed his face on the net, trying to look for the bird from the corner of his eyes, but the bird had already flown away. In his little thoughts, he wondered if he was alone, just like the time when he had to play alone when Rupan, his only friend, had gone to visit his grandparents. How he was bored and had nothing to do but take some sugar out next to the ant colony and watch them take those white flakes to their home. He wondered if even ants drank tea like his parents or his neighbour uncle did.

"Akash? Akash?"

"Yes, ma?"

"I hope you are not creating any mess?"

"No, ma…"

Akash, out of curiosity, would orchestrate minor mischiefs. Once he had put an entire slate up his nose and managed to break it inside, which almost had him killed. If it weren't for the uncle next door, who was luckily on a day off, he and his wife came investigating when they heard Akash cry. Akash's mother had already made several attempts to pluck the slate with the help of the tweezers, which further set it deeper.

Uncle Baruwa was a tobacco consumer; most of the time, he would either be crushing or chewing tobacco. He was a quick-witted man, hence he took his tobacco and stuffed it in the unblocked nostril of Akash, which made him sneeze so hard that he ended up sneezing out the slate as well. Ever since, his mother rarely left him alone, and when she had to, she would keep calling his name until he responded.

Adults lose their ability to imagine with their age, where their imaginative part is jumbled up and lost amongst the practical and calculative segments of how they live. Or perhaps they forbid the proper perspective towards life; for whatever reason, humans become miserable with the passing of each day. Unknowingly their entire existence becomes a mere *"pass-time"* as they await death.

Akash wondered if he could ever fly, Akash then imagined himself to be the very sparrow, he allowed himself to slide into a reverie, he mounted the highest footing that was the top of the pillow pile, he spread his wings and glided towards the sky.

He took off and saw the blue horizon with white patches for a moment and in the next, he witnessed the floor coming at his face with great speed, unlike his sparrow friend he came down to earth way quicker than imagined, all he remembered is a loud bang and a sharp pain on the left side of his face, no sensations beyond it, he heard footsteps of his ma, rushing towards him from the storeroom.

He tried to stand up, but the latent effect of the fall had the better of him. Akash feared being thrashed by his mother, hence he tried his best not to cry, despite all the pain. His mother picked him up and asked,

"What happened?"

"Are you hurt somewhere?"

He just shook his head, maybe because of his birthday, he was forgiven. His mother massaged his head and hugged him. This moment of maternal affection aided Akash to conjure the physical agony he was going through. Echoing between the four walls, he wailed his heart out with a loud cry.

We humans are indeed fascinating; we might be stern as rocks at the face of fear, but they melt away with the tenderness of affection. His mother rubbed his head and hugged him; he dug his face in her lap and cried. Akash's mother would usually finish making breakfast by 8:00 am, which was close to the time that Akash's father would arrive. She covered the chapati and the omelette with a plate and took Akash to visit the Gurdwara for his birthday.

His father was already home by the time Akash and Amma had returned. He was wiping himself after a shower, he saw the silhouette of the duo and turned around in excitement, "*Happy birthday, my boy!*" Akash still had a red ear and a lump on his temple above his eyes, "*What happened to my boy? Were you being naughty?*"

Akash shook his head and removed his hands from his pocket, and raised it towards his father's face;

"*Aarey? What is this? Why is your hand so messy?*"

Akash smiled and opened his little fingers and presented the KADA prashad to his father and said I saved it for you, his father could only smile. Akash was advised not to put anything greasy or sticky into his pockets as the prashad from year-old Dushera had left a stain in his new pants.

Akash was made to sit on the bed, and his father then lit the diya and put vermilion on Akash's forehead. He never liked it, it got itchy and the colour would stay for days, despite him trying his best to rub it off.

He watched his father fish his pockets and patiently waited for his gifts.

He felt butterflies inside his tummy as he anticipated his birthday gift, and then suddenly father stopped and smirked, and then extended his fist tightly clenched towards Akash. The little kid's excitement knew no bounds at the given moment, he jumped and extended both of his little palms forward and said a big "*THANK YOU, APPA!*"

His father released his fist, and down it came to Akash's palms. It was, *"one, two, thlee… thlee lupeez? (three rupees)"*. Just enough to purchase his best-loved biscuit! Akash forgets his pain, dances and runs out towards the small shop across the field. His mother gives a quick glance at her husband and Akash's father nodded. That was the last change in the name of money at their home, the rice was almost over, and they had three potatoes left, and the salary would only be credited after a day.

Akash extended his arms and ran swiftly towards the *"Dukan-wale-uncle."* He placed the three rupees on his wooden counter and said, *"Parle-G"*. *"So you came alone today, be careful as you go back."* Akash put the packet of biscuit into his pocket, turned around and ran with an equal pace towards his home, but his small lungs ran short of breath and he started to walk, ultimately leading him to rest on the log next to the paddy fields.

With eyes full of dreams, he looked up towards the vastness of the blue sky, slid his hands into the pocket and giggled. How he couldn't wait to open that packet of biscuit and share it with his ma and appa and eat the rest of them, one per day! After he felt better and his breath had stabilised, Akash got up, dusted his pants, and pushed the packet of biscuits back into his pocket, securing it as deep as he could, not realising that he had created a hole in the right-hand side pocket. He accidentally dropped the biscuit at the edge of the fields.

His reverie was disrupted as he heard some weird sound coming from the field, and the tall grasses began to move as though someone walked in his direction. This hassled him, and Akash sought to get down into the field, but he suddenly heard a grumpy grumbling of some beast. Chills went down his spine and he mustered the courage to reach out to the packet of biscuit but, a fiercely attempted bite with a bark almost, tore his hand off.

Akash fell back in shock and crawled backwards, the beast exposed itself, it was a dog, a miserable dog, its stomach had almost touched its spine and its ribs could almost be seen through its thin skin and fur, its nipples dangled abnormally and it had an intent to kill in its eyes. The beast began to growl and move towards Akash. Fortunately, this was when the milkman who was passing by stopped his bicycle, screamed and began pelting stones at the dog, forcing it to retreat.

The dog left but took the packet of biscuit along with it. Akash's clothes were dirty and he ran home crying, his face looked almost brown with dust, only streaks of his tears and snot left a mark on his face. His father was already asleep and his mother was preparing kheer in the kitchen.

At the door, he began to cry, which woke his father up, and mother rushed in from the kitchen to inquire. Akash cried out loud, fear, disappointment, rage, agony too much a little heart could handle. His father woke up and slowly turned towards him and his mother asked him, what had happened?

His parents understood, his father hugged him, and mother just stared from the ajar kitchen door with watery eyes. Indeed there is only so much a little human heart could conceive.

He could only utter two words through his sobs and hiccups.

...Dog

...Biscuit.

QUARANTINED

The people had started to slaughter their own kind for fodder and all necessary supplies. The world outside lay in pandemonium, burning in utmost agony and anguish. Rather, a self-inflicted havoc would not spare anyone—neither a long tooth nor a wean. It was a mere reflection of human greed for more power, which led time to race towards the extinction of the greatest and wisest of viruses (humans).

It had almost been three years now since this new pandemic was announced post the 2020's pandemic outbreak, which had claimed millions of lives. The world government was knocked for a loop this instant, with minimum to no time to react. It had only been announced on 03/05/2043 and, in only a span of weeks, the virus had plagued nations, killing double the number of lives, more than the last one. The incubation was not necessarily one week, as suggested by the government. Now, the occurrence of symptoms would mean death almost instantly.

All thanks to technological advancements and even faster modes of transport. The only difference this time was it was fabricated in a lab. A bio-weapon that even undermined its own creator. World government ran out of its wit! As the whole world fell into crisis just in a matter of days, the last pandemic had cost them more than ever to recover in a century. Whereas this new pandemic hung over the world like a freshly sharpened sword. It had only been four and a half decades since Corona had phased. Hence, it was as if God, once worshipped by the ignorant humans, had forsaken its creation. The divine had given up and left its creation to its fate. For the doom was inevitable this time. Most of the population was infected and dead; the remaining ones would sooner or later murder each other.

Prayash: *"It's day 342... 42... 42, no, no, wait it's day 3... 56... No, no, wait, sshhhhhh! sssshhhh! I know! I said! I know, don't say it! I said don't say it I know! It's day 36... 4 Ahhhh!"*

Prayash slammed the knife on the chopping board and toppled the half-chopped meat pieces along with the chopping board. It flew off in a dramatic fashion. It all started with a mere mouth ulcer; a calm and gentle surgeon now turned into a grouchy, deformed individual. He rather had seeped into a bit of an aggressive and unstable being, for he himself felt it! Petty things such as excessively bright daylight and loud noises would have an adverse effect on his attitude. This could have been a result of all the meat eating, as the other food resources depleted.

Prayash: *"It's okay! It's okay, (with his half frowned and enacted smirk) at least we are together, right dear?"*

He glared from the darkness of the kitchen into a half-lit dining hall towards his wife. A perfect gleam of light from the disintegrated, half-ajar window befell just too exquisitely on the tip of her nose and slightly lighter shade marginally illuminating her visage. A soothing beam, complimented by an equally placid posture that might even tranquilise the most notorious of hellhounds. There she sat smiling on a neat stool with an extraordinarily long yet clean and crisp, blue and white striped tunic that almost covered her barefoot.

Nothing was left unbroken in the room, the result of his anxiety attacks and an outburst of momentary angst. The blood-stained walls projected a violent swedge, water stained, and a loosely hung dusty calendar, half of it torn to shreds, which dated two years back from the present day.

Although there was a whole wide world that was waiting to devour them, as cannibalism had now become a common practice, *the world seemed no less than a version of hell*; In the world of the living, while on the contrary, there was no fire to be burnt alive as its biblical counterpart, but rather brute savagery and the primordial instinct of humans to survive.

Prayash: "*Oh! Just look at your perfect smile, isn't it one thing to live for or rather to die for.*" (Prayash stressed "*to die for*".)

Prayash slowly rested his mutilated head on his wife's lap, smiling in mitigation, and with a half-bruised back, acquired from his last encounter with the other savages of his own species. He went out for supplies and ran into a scavenger group; it was a narrow escape. He never broke a word in front of Shanti, nor did she ask; she hardly spoke a word after the incident, where Prayash had miraculously revived her from the dead.

He sluggishly got on his knees and dug deep into her lap. He heavily sighed and took a deep breath; his lungs were instantly filled with the scent of Rhododendron. It was almost a dismissal of all the havoc. He felt his pain gradually subsided, and now were a thing of the past. He slid into a surreal nostalgia slightly…

…warm rays, preferably a shade that of a ripe peach befell him. A snooping cold breeze brushed his hair as he lay on the dirt. When he opened his eyes he no longer lay on the same dirt but rather on a crisp dew-filled, grass field, probably the hills of Tonglu. He now lay face up on his beloved Shanti's lap, looking at her radiant face, which had nothing more but adoration and gratitude to offer. A million questions flew through his conscience.

"Where were they? Why was it so peaceful? Who was he? Where was his undying resentment and anger?"

Almost as if an ant would think if offered a conscience of their own, yet still out of all the other questions, only 'one' seemed important, and that kept on drifting through his conscience.

Prayash: *"Shanti, do you remember the first time we met?"*

She smiled as she always did, and gently nodded a yes, soft wind still gently stroking their hair as their eyes constantly rested on each other. He could hear keys of a piano faintly ringing in the distance. Prayash could barely make it out, *Sonata no.2, III* (funeral march).

He looked at his palm; his hands were soft and spongy again, just as they used to be when things were normal. But this wasn't normal! Stuck by a certain sense of reality, he tried to lift himself; his body felt rather stiff and rigid as if he was asleep. Prayash tried to wake up and shake this heavy weight off his chest. In the end, giving up, he blinked his eyes a couple of times, held them shut for a longer period.

He now heard the *Sonata* much clearer, as one would see through a freshly cleaned windowpane. Now much relaxed and relieved, he decided to surrender to this sensation of sleep paralysis and, after one more clutch on his eyelids. To his astonishment, he himself was playing the *Sonata*. Taken aback, Prayash fell from the stool, pressing the base notes and onto Shanti's bosom. She lulled him with those cavernous hazel brown eyes and smile, once again instilling the calm in him.

Shanti: *"I remember the first time we met Prayash, it was on the way to my concert, and we had to share the taxi... we met in that cab."*

Prayash: *"Yes, that black cab 0094, the only day I regretted sitting in the front seat."*

Shanti: *"Why would you say that?"*

Prayash: *"Isn't it obvious, because you sat there on the second seat, it drizzled gently with the drops remaining stagnant on the window pane, the world outside was dark for the daylight was hidden in that black taxi."*

Shanti: *"Oh, you are very cheesy!"*

Prayash smiled and she laughed. A perfect wrinkle formed on her nose that made her look even more admirable, carefree and captivating. All that Prayash could do was stare at her and helplessly smile, enchanted by her immensely enriching aura. He thought to himself how beautiful it would be if time stopped right where they were.

Prayash heard distant bangs, which became louder and clearer each time, it came so much closer to him that he felt his eardrums would rupture wide open. Finally waking him up from his deep and much-needed sleep. The room that Prayash had transcended from seemed even darker and was now replaced by pale moonbeams. His throat felt dry with dehydration, lips cracked open. A rugged voice pierced the momentary silence of the dark…

Voice 1: "*We know you are hiding in there, you punk!*"

A secondary voice, feeble, trailed in a pleasing manner, seeking validation.

Voice 2: "*Aye, punk, we will make you pay for what you did! You better come out! We are here to get you, right boss?*" (Almost eating up his own words.)

With great effort, Prayash lifted himself up and grabbed his gun, checking the last remaining four bullets in his coat's pocket and loaded them into the revolver. He carried Shanti to the master bedroom and asked her to remain quiet in the wardrobe, he begged her not to come out whatsoever.

He then grabbed the water bottle and drank as steadily as he could with his shaky, weak hands. Prayash rushed to the kitchen, grabbed the blood-stained cleaver and hid himself inside the dismantled dusty couch. All this while, those voices were trying to break into the house. He peeped through the tatty end of the couch until they finally broke in with three gunshots near the

handle. He saw four tall and broad figures and one slightly shorter and leaner as they barged into his apartment hall, disintegrating the main door, raising the dust clouds. They were armed with knives and wooden planks. Prayash vaguely saw as the dust clouds gradually settled, strangely they covered their mouths and kept complaining of a foul smell similar to that of a rotting carcass. The same rugged voice commanded;

Voice 1: "*Look for that swine! Try and catch him alive, I shall kill him slowly bit by bit, by plucking his nails and chopping him up all this while he is still conscious. Try getting rid of that smell too, it's making me sick.*"

Spitting towards the couch, he understood it was the same set of scavengers that he had encountered earlier today. The statement alone sent chills down his spine; he became more alert and aggressive with every inhale and exhale as his heart pumped adrenaline through his veins. From almost one drop at a time, he began to sweat like a pig, his palms became very sweaty. He had to wipe them on his shirt again and again. His body now began to shiver with rage. It went up to his eyes, turning them red and bloodshot.

Despite all this, he clung on to the very last ounce of sanity that remained in him. Prayash began his calculations and his plan of attack; protecting Shanti from the trespassers was his sole purpose. All this while, he lay inside his shabby couch, calculating while his trespassers turned his guest room upside down, looking for him.

Voice 2: "*This room is clear! Manish, we found some gold!*"

"*What will you do with that? Look for that lunatic and some food and let's get out of here!*"

Manish: "*Let's check the kitchen!*"

The shorter and leaner figure was in the lead, now with a tiny pen torch in his hand, something that they probably found moments ago while scavenging. He was followed by three other bulkier figures that held knives and were trying to look around as they checked the bathroom and the storeroom. Breaking this stereotypical silence, the shorter figure came out running and screaming at the top of his squeaky and shaky voice. The other men gathered around him.

Manish: "*What is it, kid? Did you get him?!*"

Now his face was much more visible with the moonbeam that ran across the room. He was just a kid, no more than fifteen or sixteen, with shabby clothes, messy dusky hair, and a barely visible peach fuzz above his lips. His wide eyes remained wide open even after he came out, with an open jaw and shivering body. His eyes, wide and still, depicted the true horror he had witnessed inside.

The men who went inside the kitchen laughed nervously as their friend lay in pieces on the kitchen floor and counter. They rushed outside to tell Manish what they had seen, but it was already too late. They saw him lying in a pool of blood with a slit throat and multiple stab wounds on his back. Three of them stayed stunned while the kid sat on the floor where he was left. One of them ran towards him and asked,

"Kid, did you see who did this?" violently shaking him again.

"I said, who did this?! Answer me!" slapping him this time.

"We shouldn't be here! We should have left him alone!" the kid replied in a very feeble and shaky voice.

"Did you see where he went?"

The kid weakly pointed towards the bedroom while the other two now rushed in and said, *"Let's search this place and put an end to this!"*

Voice 3: *"Bubu, you stay with the kid!"*

The two men rushed inside the bedroom, one of them holding a Glock and the other holding a Mossberg, pointing it towards the old door aligned horizontally to his shoulder. As soon as the other one opened the bathroom door, a bright flash of light pierced through the darkness, shattering the silence. A loud gunshot fired at point-blank range left the man dead, with his hand still clinging to the doorknob and his brains blown out on the bathroom door. He lay there lifeless. The other man ran in and started shooting randomly everywhere, screaming wildly.

"Now I see you, rat! You are nothing but dead meat now!"

Prayash fired one round in retaliation, managing to wound one of them as he heard one cry in pain. The wounded man was eventually dragged out of the room, leaving only one man in pursuit. Prayash had his left hand blown away, which was still holding onto the revolver. It must have been a shotgun that he had miscalculated for a wooden beam. Prayash hurriedly pulled hydrogen peroxide from the side table, sat down, biting on his knees, and poured it on the remaining half of his forearm. His grunt was low and feeble.

He caught his cleaver with his right hand and charged like a cornered lion, striking the tallest man on the nape and instantly killing him, further stabbing him to ensure he was dead. He killed the other man by stabbing him in the heart. The kid ran inside, screaming, and grabbed whatever his hands could grasp, pointing it towards Prayash.

Prayash had become much calmer. He smiled and stood up with great effort, limping towards the kid with blood still dripping from his left arm. Calling it the kid's bluff, Prayash tried to close in. The kid kept walking backwards in trepidation until, finally, with his back against the wall, he slid down and rested helplessly on the floor. A loud thunderclap-like sound…

The room was lit for a split second, and then it all fell silent, filled with the stench of blood, rotting meat, sweat, and gunpowder. The night restored its calm again. A soft wind blew through a hole in the window frame, creating a wheezing sound. Prayash slowly lifted his arm to deliver the final blow, but the ground came towards his face as he lost his balance. He lay face down on the dirt; it was a bullet shot from his revolver. The bullet was shot from such an angle that it punctured his lungs and managed to rupture his oesophagus. He saw a bright flash, heard a loud bang, and simultaneously felt a sharp pain in his lower back, along with a few clicks in an attempt to empty the whole cylinder.

Prayash: *"It's over, kid, it's over…You've done it."* (With great effort and a gargling voice)

Prayash now finally came back to his senses, with his adrenaline leaking out with his blood, creating a pool. The pain became more intense, but the kid had already left Prayash to his demise and ran away. He dragged himself towards the wardrobe and opened it to bid his wife a final farewell, but instead, a decaying corpse fell on top of him, infested with maggots, with few strands of hair remaining on the scalp and hollow eye sockets. It was a corpse almost in the final stage of decay, all that remained of his beautiful Shanti.

This was the final restoration of his senses and sanity. Recalling the day when they had gone out for supplies and were attacked by a large horde of savages. In a desperate attempt to escape, he had run his car into a tree, which threw Shanti off her seat as she hit her head on the windshield, instantly killing her with a ruptured skull.

Prayash wept in a hush and tried to smile, recalling their rudimentary promises. They always spoke of living and dying together. Although she left him sooner, she patiently waited for him without any rush or complaints. Prayash's eyes filled as he took his final breaths, and he continued playing the Sonata in the air while lying next to Shanti.

LUKE

Before we begin, one may refer to me as the void. You only notice my presence in my absence, and without me all is mundane. Now, onward with the story…

Far above the busy, humid, and hot mainlands, that are filled with loud noises, honks, and where no individual can be heard with ease, at the lap of mountains sits a small town, Ghoom. When inquired, the place is often ridiculed for its gloomy and cold atmosphere, but rarely would they know that a Ghoom after rain or a bright summer day feels like the fairytale of elves. Fresh air, luscious green trees, flowers grown and decorated on every balcony, smiley and inquisitive faces, a concave view of the land of orchids, hills, and mountains where birds sing in both high and low notes.

Patches of fog climb uphill with bits and essence being stuck on the majestic and proud pinewood trees, although the strands of cotton would get stuck on the bed strap. Yet, from the aft of Tiger Hill mountain, a dark nimbus looks down upon Ghoom. As we close in on this particular house, we can see an earthworm struggling in a small drain, wrestling against this alien slimy froth. Some could even hear it scream, "as the legends suggest," while it struggles in this life-and-death battle. A little boy scoots down and watches it closely in awe, holding a toothbrush in his hand and a cup of water in the other, and we shall call him Luke.

"*Luke! How long will you take to brush your teeth? It's been ten minutes already, your breakfast is getting cold!*" (That would be Luke's mother, and we will refer to her as Auntie J)

"*News of crisis everywhere, global warming, murders, rapes, mob lynching, theft, job crisis.*" (This is his cousin, a troubled young man who thinks the world is an important place. We shall refer to him as Dada.)

Auntie J: "*Why do you even read that piece of paper if you do not like it?*"

Dada: "*To know…*"

Auntie J: "*I do not understand what you would do with that amount of irrelevant information.*"

Dada: "*I shall discuss them in class.*"

Auntie J: "*Why not look for proper jobs instead, you are already in your late 20s, it is about time.*"

Meanwhile, Luke wipes his face as he sluggishly sits at the dining table and waits for the adults to finish their part of the irrelevant and unimportant discussion, as he looks from one end to the other.

Luke: "*Hey Dada, good morning, you know what day it is? AND YOU KNOW WHO IS GOING TO COME?*"

Dada: "*No.*"

Luke: "*AVINAB DADA!*"

Dada: "*Well, someone is going to have fun today, even the day looks bright, just like your mood!*"

But the clouds might have instilled some mischief, with the sole purpose of ruining Luke's plans! Practical grownups rarely have plans as they are aware that seldom will things snowball as they have been planned. Most of the time, neither the dreams are fulfilled nor the plans are met. But children break this mundane spell of existence; they fail to understand, rather they choose to defy, or perhaps they even dare to get upset. Do we become more miserable as we grow old because we become more logical, or is it because one suspends and disproves one's inner child?

This was a small conversation between small people with big/small problems. In actuality, no one knows, nothing really matters, but there must be something that keeps one from giving up and entails that ounce of courage to rise up and push through another day. Humans are indeed an interesting species and a larger-than-mortal-life subject. They live a sequential repeated telecast of the previous day with minor adjustments, just enough for them to realise, until they meet the end.

Little Luke rejoiced at the thought of his future revere, where he plans on having a perfect weekend with his friend Avinab Dada, who is supposed to visit him later in the day. Let us see and learn what the day has instilled for us, as we move forward.

Auntie J: "*Luke, you have to take a bath, come here and take off your clothes, now!*"

Luke: "*Alright, I'm coming…*"

This has become a drill now. Every weekend little Luke takes off his clothes in a wimpy fashion as his daily shower in Mumbai has turned into a weekly shower, due to comparatively colder weather and lesser outdoor activities. He bangs his feet, throwing tantrums, making it obvious that he does not fancy a clean-up, especially when his friends are showing up to play. Meanwhile, the dark nimbus has climbed up the hill a little higher. As the chilly winds fetch the message of some forgotten lover from the Sandakphu range and send the reverberations of their lover's betrayal down one's spine.

Luke has a tan complexion, curly hair like his mother's, a big bone structure, a fascinating charm, chinky eyes, and a heart-melting smile, which looks quite notorious when he plots mischief. One knows that he is planning mischief when his eyes twinkle, with his gap-filled smirk as his milk tooth fell off just last week. He is smart for his age.

It was only last week he surprised his Dada by wishing for the well-being of the entire world, as he explained his wish when enquired. His Dada, although an atheist, likes to visit religious places, and he took Luke to visit the not-so-famous yet oldest monastery in Darjeeling, the Yiga Choeling Monastery. Dada relayed what was told to him as a kid, that Luke could make a wish by pelting a stone at the top of the wish-making pagoda. If his pelted stone stayed, his wish would come true.

It has been a week since I heard that wish, and this boy draws my inquisitiveness. Luke's excitement rages, and he begins to jump as they close in towards the latter half of the day.

Luke: *"Yael Lunchtime, and after that, you know what time it is, Dada?"*

Dada: *"No."*

Dada playfully replied. He wonders how children are gifted with this present of forgetfulness, concluding perhaps it was a result of his outpouring of excitement.

Lunch was ready and his friend's visit was only thirty minutes away. He couldn't wait for the time to pass and kept on checking the time with his immaculate eyes. He savoured the food, however, his attention was more on the clock today. With momentary glances around the quiet faces of the dining table, he couldn't stop smiling at his grandfather and Dada with his mischievous yet serene eyes.

What a lovely place, time, and age to be. The clouds by now had invaded the sky above Ghoom, and the fog had perfectly dampened the green moss and the pinewood trees. The clouds began to rumble and the night prevailed over broad daylight, and the weather gleaned the entire room. Unsolicited cold moisture seeped through the walls, silence became prominent, and disappointment manifested itself in physical essence. With a shaky voice, as the downpour began…

Luke: *"Ma, Avinab Dada will come, right?"*

Auntie J: *"No, baba, it's pouring outside, how will he come?"*

Luke: "No, *but he promised he'd come… He will come, he will have to come. He said he will come!*"

Auntie J: "*Luke!*"

This was enough for him to quiet down, but by the time he had finished his third sentence, his eyes had already welled up, and with a mouthful of his chicken rice, he began to cry at the top of his voice, such an uncommon reason to be sad. His tiny heart must have hurt as he stood in complete denial. Steaming food, the musty smell from the soaked wooden objects, and vivid sobs of Luke, with momentary lightning and thunder outside. While Grandfather was a man of few words. He added,

Grandfather: "*Now, now, it's okay, he will come once the rain stops. Till then you finish your food and prepone your screen time.*"

Auntie J: "*Luke, if you don't stop, you'll have it from me. Finish your food, fast.*"

Grandmother: "*Don't scold the poor child, he will be here in no time.*"

…as she finishes her last sip of Churpi-ko-Jhol (fermented cottage cheese soup), I add to it,

Grandmother: "*Yes, if not, I'll go get him, as soon as it stops raining.*"

"A heart wants what it wants, what it wants," especially when it comes down to the younger minds. The zeal and stubbornness that they possess is envy-worthy. Grandmother fetches two A4-sized papers from her room and starts folding it. She puts down a few folds and looks at Dada.

Grandmother: "*Do you still remember how to make a boat?*"

Dada: "*I believe I do…*"

As the paper overlaps and begins to take the shape of a boat, both Grandmother and Dada begin to sing, "*Row, row, row your boat…*"

Grandmother sings in Nepali and Dada in English. They both tap into their inner child, or nostalgia perhaps, and Luke joins them from the second verse and attempts folding a piece of paper along. Grandfather gets up, switches on the light, and leaves for his room. A bright room, nostalgic song, steam from the kettle, empty plates, and the aroma of warm kheer. Luke smiles again. His interest is sparked yet again.

Luke: "*Is that for me, Dada?*"

Dada: "*Yes, Luke.*"

Luke: "*Oh, wow, so cool! So, can I play with it in the water?*"

Dada: "*Yes, Luke.*"

Luke: "*So, it won't get wet and fall off?*"

Auntie J: "*Luke, let him finish! How many questions will you ask him?*"

Dada: "*It might get wet and drown, Luke, everything eventually does, but you know what?*"

Luke: "*What, Dada?*"

Dada: "*We shall make another one! Because we are seafaring pirates, and what do the pirates say?*"

Luke: "*Yes, we are! ARRRRR!*"

He grasped Grandmother's hand with his little fingers and the boat with the other, sat next to the tub, and began singing as soon as he placed his boat on the water. It rode the waves formed by his little hand, and it mused to the melody. Tarpaulin fluttered above him, his half-wet sleeve, and a smile to even melt the rock. Everyone else returned to their mundane activities: cleaning, feeding pets, washing, and mopping. But Luke had a eureka moment!

Luke: "*Dada, I have an excellent idea! Let us make planes.*"

Planes it was. He also wanted boats, but planes more. In a moment, he became a pirate to a brave space pirate. He certainly had fought a kraken in his paper boat and now he wanted to slay a space dragon with his "supersonic aircraft." Dada managed to fold a paper plane from his rusty memory. There was once a time when he used to fly those paper planes, thinning out the workbooks to their spine. The boats sailed the most dangerous drains. There was a time where 'now' just passed by under one's attention. Little Luke lives there now, on his own now.

As he ran out to fly his plane, the clouds had finally relayed their burden and only petrichor-infused, cold fresh air blew from time to time. The sun rested towards the horizon, reflecting a breathtaking double rainbow above a neatly washed Tiger Hill. It had washed off its human sins. The wind offered a perfect lift to Luke's plane, and it flew, forcing Luke to jump with joy. He let go of the plane as he let go of the boat, and now he demanded a new plane. His friend Avinab was at the door. Luke pulled out his Lego and Hot Wheels set and no longer required the plane which he demanded a moment ago.

Thus, if there is anyone capable of forgetting and letting go of me so easily, it must be such a child of kind heart and pure, harmless intent, the embodiment of inquisitiveness. Luke, in doing so, acts as the quintessence of the most complex enigma of existence, the manner of living and not just existing. No object or feeling of joy or remorse is permanent, but rather, existence itself is in a constant flow. It never waits, it never rests, it flows.

The grown-up world is not wrong to expect, but neither are they right when one disapproves of the things that matter. One is ought to denounce their desire in search of peace, but what are beings even without desires, certainly not humans. Thus, the answer lies in letting go…

I shall leave you with this small tale of a small boy from this mystical place as I wander around the world seeking more stories as such!

P.S. - "*Vivamus Moriendum est*"

INDEX

Ama: Mother

Pao: Famous bread made of all-purpose flour in Mumbai

Banyan: Tank-top/undershirt

Murda: Low stool made using bamboo and animal skin

Chula: A kitchen set, prepared with rocks and red soil

Sotey: Blowpipe

Parde-topi: Nepali cultural hat made out of cloth

Dhaura sural: Traditional Nepali attire

Dhero: Flour cooked by simply adding water and stirring it
until it turns into a dry gooey substance

Daju/Dada: Brother

Fika-cheya: Black tea, ideally served with sugar or salt

Doko: Basket made out of bamboo strips

Phuli: Gold ornament made by beating it into the shape of
a flower

Haat bajar: Flea market

Bhutey ko mula ko sag: Sautéed radish leaves

9 798889 475004